A Song
for
Bijou

ALSO BY JOSH FARRAR

Rules to Rock By

A Song for Bijou

JOSH FARRAR

WALKER BOOKS FOR YOUNG READERS
AN IMPRINT OF BLOOMSBURY
NEW YORK   LONDON   NEW DELHI   SYDNEY

Copyright © 2013 by Josh Farrar
All rights reserved. No part of this book may be reproduced or transmitted in any form
or by any means, electronic or mechanical, including photocopying, recording, or by any
information storage and retrieval system, without permission in writing from the publisher.

First published in the United States of America in February 2013
by Walker Books for Young Readers, an imprint of Bloomsbury Publishing, Inc.
www.bloomsbury.com

For information about permission to reproduce selections from this book, write to
Permissions, Walker BFYR, 175 Fifth Avenue, New York, New York 10010

Library of Congress Cataloging-in-Publication Data
Farrar, Josh.
A song for Bijou / Josh Farrar.
p.   cm.
Summary: Seventh-grader Alex Schrader's life changes when he meets Bijou Doucet, a
Haitian girl recently relocated to Brooklyn, and while he is determined to win her heart
Alex also learns about dating rules and Haitian culture.
ISBN 978-0-8027-3394-8 (hardcover) • ISBN 978-0-8027-3395-5 (ebook)
[1. Interpersonal relationships—Fiction.   2. Dating (Social customs)—Fiction.
3. Preparatory schools—Fiction.   4. Schools—Fiction.   5. Haitian Americans—
Fiction.   6. Brooklyn (New York, N.Y.)—Fiction.]   I. Title.
PZ7.F2432So 2013   [Fic]—dc23   2012027537

Book design by Nicole Gastonguay
Typeset by Westchester Book Composition
Printed in the U.S.A. by Thomson-Shore, Dexter, Michigan
2 4 6 8 10 9 7 5 3 1

All papers used by Bloomsbury Publishing, Inc., are natural, recyclable products
made from wood grown in well-managed forests. The manufacturing processes
conform to the environmental regulations of the country of origin.

For Tayef

A Song for Bijou

 1

The Slow-Motion Thing

The first time I see her, following Mary Agnes Brady out of Peas n' Pickles at 3:47 on a Wednesday afternoon in the second week of March, the slow-motion thing happens. It's like the pause button's been pushed on everything I see. The image—a beautiful girl with butterfly braids, snapping back the tab on a can of ginger ale—freezes for a millisecond. After the sound of the can's sharp pop and the little breath of fizz that follows it, time stops, and I think, *Who is that incredible girl?*

Then the picture comes to life again, but slowly, one frame at a time, as if an invisible thumb has pushed play without unpausing. So slowly that I don't miss a single detail: from the mist of carbonation that sprays into the air and disappears, to the puzzled look on the girl's face as she pulls the inch-long paper wrapper off the bent tip of the straw, to the shy smile that spreads across her face as she takes the first sip. Then she says, "Mmm," and she licks her lips like she's never tasted ginger ale in her life.

Nomura and I are in a long line of kids from St. Cat's and St. Chris's, waiting to pay for our food, and Mary Agnes is walking out of the store backward, like a tour guide, pointing to snacks near the cash register and explaining the names, prices, and pros and cons of 3 Musketeers, Fuji apples, and Fritos. She enunciates each syllable, as if speaking to a child or someone hard of hearing. The girl doesn't seem to mind, though. She's paying close attention, nodding every few seconds, hungry for information.

Her uniform is brand-new. Her shirt, its collar stiff with starch, is whiter than Mary Agnes's, and not only because it stands out against her skin. Her red plaid skirt is brighter, too, and her patent-leather saddle shoes are as shiny as mirrors, not a scratch on them. Every piece of clothing on her looks like it was bought in the last forty-eight hours.

As usual, Mary Agnes is talking nonstop, and the girl looks like she has to concentrate to keep up. Every time she nods, her braids do a little dance, shimmying like a grass skirt, before coming to rest. At the end of each braid sits a tiny purple bead in the shape of a butterfly. I wonder if she twists her hair into braids herself or if someone has to do it for her. I wonder whether she can sleep with the beads on. And, if she took the butterflies off, would the braids unravel?

I don't normally notice stuff like this. I only do when the slow-motion thing happens. Which is not something I choose or have any control of whatsoever. Someone else is controlling it. It's like God, or somebody, is saying, *Pay attention. This is important!*

Time speeds up again, although I feel like I'm still two seconds behind. "Who's that?" I whisper to Nomura.

He doesn't even hear me. I have to say it twice because he's reading something on his phone and dipping into a bag of Utz chips we haven't paid for yet.

"Who's who?" he answers at last, his lips forming a round "o." Everything about Nomura is round. His moon-shaped face, his black bowl-cut hair—even his glasses—are all circles so perfect they look like they've been drawn with a compass.

"Do you want a microphone?" I whisper, praying none of the girls can hear us. Nomura is as loud as he is circular.

Mary Agnes is still lecturing the girl. "The black girl?" he asks. "I don't know. I've never seen her before."

I pay for Nomura's chips and my Butterfinger, and Mr. Lau, the old man who owns Peas n' Pickles, slaps my change on the counter like he's placing a bet in a Chinese poker game. Then, a loud metal-on-Formica slap: the girls are out

the door already. Too fast for me to say hello, or to do anything else that will help me meet that beautiful girl.

"She must be new," I say. "We would have seen her
before."

"She's cute," Nomura says. "*Really* cute."

"I saw her first."

"Slow down, cowboy. All I said was she's cute. But if you
want to chase after her, go right ahead. She's out of your
league, and she'll probably break your heart into a million
pieces, but if that's what you're after, she's all yours."

By the time we're out of the store, though, the girls are
past Pineapple Street, probably on their way to the subway.
They're walking in regular time, their hard-heeled shoes
clicking musically against the concrete, nothing slo-mo
about it. But I know that something has happened, something worth paying attention to. Something *monumental*.

I need to find out who that girl is, where she came
from, and why I've never seen her before, even though
Nomura and I know, or at least know *of*, all forty-four girls
in the seventh- and eighth-grade classes at St. Catherine's
School for Girls.

Somehow I know that the answers to these questions
are going to change my life forever.

2

What's Wrong with All-Boys Schools, Pt. 1

St. Christopher makes getting to know girls almost impossible. Well, maybe not St. Christopher himself, whoever he was. But St. Christopher's, the school where I've been going for eight endless years. St. Christopher's School for Boys in Brooklyn Heights, New York City.

Honestly, what is the point of a boys-only school in the twenty-first century? Maybe it made sense in 1913, when this place was founded. When half the boys at St. Chris's wanted to become monks or priests—two jobs that make you swear off girls for life—when they grew up. But now, a hundred years later, I can promise you that none of the guys I know has ever once thought about giving up girls for good just so he can serve God. And what's so holy and spiritual about completely ignoring half the people on Earth, anyway?

If you ask me, it's sexist.

Some people say that single-sex schools help kids concentrate better, but that's crazy. I would never want to look like an idiot in front of a whole bunch of cute girls, so I would study even harder if St. Chris's were coed. I'd memorize my entire Latin textbook (and this is a completely different subject, but where else do you have to learn Latin, except inside the walls of an all-boys school?) if it meant I had a chance to impress a room half filled with members of the fairer sex.

I'd be way less depressed, too. Have you ever looked at the seventh- and eighth-grade classes in a boys school and seen how bummed out everyone looks? More than half my class has been at St. Chris's since kindergarten. That includes me; my best friend, John Nomura; my other friend, Ira Lopez; Richard Krug; Greg Vargas; Rocky Van Sant; Trevor Zelo; and a few others, and let me tell you: we are so completely sick of one another that we are miserably depressed. And who wouldn't be? Imagine looking at the same boring faces, day after day, for eight whole years. With the exception of Nomura and Ira, if I never saw a single one of my classmates' ugly mugs again, I would die happy! And if they all, with the exception of Ira and Nomura, said the same thing about me, I wouldn't blame them.

But I'm stuck with these guys, they're stuck with me, and we're not even through seventh grade yet.

Now, if half my class were girls, things would be completely different. Sure, we'd still be sick of one another after eight whole years, but starting in sixth grade, certain miraculous biological, um, changes would become noticeable in many of us, and these changes, these transformations, would make all the difference. We'd see one another with new eyes. Friendships would change and grow, romances would blossom, and like I mentioned before, we'd all be studying really hard.

So, having girls at St. Chris's would make us all smarter and way better prepared for high school. I guarantee it.

3

Ignoramus

Thank God for the St. Catherine's dances.

If I had seen that incredible girl—I still don't know her name, but Nomura and I are working on it—in sixth grade, tracking her down without blowing my cover would have been a challenge. But because of the St. Cat's dances, I'm going to meet her, and soon. As in Saturday-night soon.

The staff at St. Chris's have never hosted a dance, thrown a party, or given any opportunity whatsoever for us to meet girls. But the people who run St. Cat's, which is our sister school and is only three blocks away, think that dances are a very big deal, and they throw them three times a year. Every girl in seventh and eighth grade goes to these "St. Cathopher's" dances, because they're as desperate to meet boys as we are to meet them. The next one, Spring Fling, is Saturday night.

The incredible girl will be there, because *everyone* will be there. And if Mary Agnes Brady has taken the girl under her wing and sees herself as the girl's personal tour guide, there's no *way* she'll miss Spring Fling, because Mary Agnes is obsessed with the dances. She lives for them.

......ℓℓℓℓℓ......

At lunch on Thursday, Nomura sidesteps a kickball game in the yard and meets me in the corner next to a play structure I haven't climbed since fifth grade. He's got Ira with him, and Ira, as always, is shooting video. I haven't seen him without that video cam of his for months.

"Her name," Nomura says, "is Bijou."

Bijou. *Bijou, Bijou, Bijou.*

I look at Nomura, then back at Ira. "And how many people did you have to ask to find out?" Nomura's not exactly a human Fort Knox when it comes to keeping secrets, but Ira's another story altogether. "I don't want people to know I'm, you know, interested."

"Me and Ira, that's it," Nomura says.

"Ira," I say, "you mind turning that thing off? Not every moment of our lives has to be on video. I don't want the world knowing about this."

"Relax, man, my work is strictly confidential." He clicks the camera off. "And nobody knows you like this girl. Nobody except Maricel, that is."

Ira has a twin sister, Maricel, at St. Cat's, but this is the first time that their relationship's been useful in any way. Maricel is smart, pretty, and even semipopular. She's also friends with Mary Agnes, so she must at least know Bijou a little bit and is probably a gold mine of information.

A little more on Ira, my second-best friend: Ira is always obsessed with something. And I do mean *obsessed*. When he dives into an interest, it's headfirst into the deep end. First it was Pokémon cards, then *Diary of a Wimpy Kid*, and then he memorized practically every line of all seventeen Harry Potter movies. These days it's horror: vampires, flesh-eating zombies, witches, shape-shifters, werewolves, even were-panthers, all of which are not only 100 percent fictional, but also way less interesting than the very real, fantastical creatures among us called *girls*. Ira couldn't care less about girls, though. All he cares about, for now, anyway, is becoming some kind of major movie director. He'd better be careful with that camera of his. I don't want everybody to know I like Bijou; that would ruin everything.

"So, what kind of name is Bijou?" I ask.

"It's French," Nomura says. "It means 'jewel.' "

"But she's not French," Ira says. He's talking really, really fast. He's so excited, he can't spit out the words fast enough. Maybe I was wrong; does Ira Lopez care about girls after all? "She's Haitian."

"Asian?" I ask.

Nomura laughs. "No, Alex. *Haitian*. As in, from *Haiti*."

I look at him blankly. "Is that in Africa?"

"No, it's not in Africa! Do you *ever* watch the news?" I give him a look; he *knows* I don't follow the news.

How many guys in our class watch the news? Only one: Nomura. And he doesn't even *watch* the news, he reads the *New York Times*, the actual physical newspaper, every morning while drinking a cup of black coffee. He brings it with him on the subway, folding it into a neat square, and sometimes he even reads it between classes. The kid is never more than ten feet away from the *Times*.

"You might remember this gigantic disaster that happened in January 2010." He looks at me like he can't even believe he's still friends with somebody as dumb as me. "The Haitian earthquake? Hello, calling Alex Schrader. . . . Is anybody in there?"

"Three years ago? How am I supposed to remember something that happened when I was ten years old?"

"I remember it," Ira says. "Haiti's an island, and the whole thing was torn to shreds. There were poor people living in tents and shacks. Crying and dying, total catastrophe."

"Oh *that*," I say. "Yeah." What I remember is Mom, close to tears, watching CNN in horror as the camera showed thousands of people with no homes, and how hot the place was, how completely miserable everyone seemed.

Then Mom used a five-digit code to text a ten-dollar dona-
tion to the Red Cross.

Not for one second could I believe that the beautiful girl
could have had anything to do with a place like that. She
looked so fresh and clean and . . . innocent. Not like somebody who's been through all of that.

"Okay, obviously I know what Haiti is," I say, feeling
the color rise to my cheeks. "I just forgot that *Haitians* were
from Haiti. *Haitian* sounds exactly like *Asian.*"

"What an ignoramus," Nomura says.

Ira giggles.

"You're so ignorant," I tell Ira, "you don't even know
what *ignoramus* means."

"Do too," Ira says. But then he shuts up, because he really
doesn't.

"So, where is it?" I ask Nomura. "Is it near Africa at
least?"

"Have you ever heard of Cuba, white boy?" Nomura asks,
getting a laugh from Ira. Nomura's Japanese and Ira's half
Dominican, so they think it's incredibly hilarious to call me
"white boy" any time I say something stupid.

"Yeah, dude, I've heard of Cuba, thank you very much."

"Haiti is south of Cuba," Ira says. "But it's right next to
the Dominican. They're on the same island . . . *ignoramus.*"
Okay, so he does know the word. Big deal.

I pretend not to hear. I don't know much about the

Dominican Republic, except that a lot of good baseball players are Dominican and that Ira isn't one of them. He's terrible at sports, the kind of kid who strikes out in kickball.

"Do you know anything else about her?" I ask him. "I mean, she wasn't in that earthquake, was she?"

"I don't know, but I can find out." Ira bites his lip.

"Awesome, Ira." I do genuinely appreciate his help. Without Maricel's info, I'd still be clueless. "Fantastic, in fact."

"Wow, Alex, you're so into this girl, it's almost scary," Nomura says.

"I'm a red-blooded adolescent male."

"You might still actually be *pre*adolescent, dude."

"It doesn't drive you half-crazy, knowing there are 243 girls only three blocks away?"

"You're obsessed," Nomura says.

"You're more into girls than I am into horror," Ira says.

"That's because girls are real and horror is lame," I say.

"Is not," says Ira.

"Seriously, Alex. It's all you ever talk about lately." Nomura balls up his lunch bag and tosses it with a perfect arc into a trash can.

"We're in seventh grade. Isn't that normal?"

"Maybe, but it seems like girls have completely taken over your life. Like it's the most important thing, ever."

Instead of saying that girls *are* the most important thing

ever, which they obviously are, I say, "Please, they haven't taken over *anything*."

"I'm not so sure about that. Let's say you were given the choice between losing us as your best friends and getting to know this girl. What would you choose?"

"He'd choose us, obviously," Ira says, looking at Nomura. Then to me, "Wouldn't you?"

"I would gladly never talk to my own sister again in exchange for a girlfriend," I reply, "if that's what you mean."

"No, I'm serious," Nomura says. "Would you choose a girl over us?"

"Of course not," I say. "How could you ask that?" And I mean it. Nomura is my best friend. And Ira is awesome, too. I would never do anything to hurt them, even if the hottest supermodel in the world were on her knees, begging me to be her husband.

"Are you sure?" Nomura asks. "Because when you talk about girls, you get this glazed look in your eyes, almost like one of Ira's zombies. You're not going to do us in, are you?"

Ira sticks his arms out like one of the undead and pretends to take a bite of my arm flesh.

"Knock it off," I say. But then, seriously, "No way. Not a chance."

"Even for Angela Gudrun?" Ira asks, knowing that only months ago, I talked about Angela every single day—every hour of every day, in fact. My Angela fixation was probably very annoying, I admit. But that was before Bijou. And now that I'm over Angela, it seems safe to respond in my goofiest pirate accent, "Ira, if I could have but one mere day with Angela Gudrun, I'd gladly say good-bye to you and Nomura, now and forevermore!"

They both crack up, which is generous, considering how weak the joke is.

"Friendship can walk the plank, matey!" I yell.

They know I don't mean it.

Cramming

It's still Friday, only three classes to go before the weekend. Nomura, Ira, and I get to seventh-grade study hall early so we can grab the table in the far corner of the library. It's the farthest one from where Mr. Blossom, the librarian, sits, so you can usually talk quietly or at least pass notes without getting in trouble.

"Do they speak English?" I whisper to Nomura. I've got the "H" volume of *Encyclopedia Britannica* in front of me—all the computer stations were taken before I got here, so I'm stuck with this monstrous book, furiously flipping the pages toward the "Haiti" entry.

"Who?" Ira asks.

"Haitians," Nomura says.

"I think they speak French," Ira says. I can't believe he knows more about Haiti than I do, but he won't for long.

"That's good," I say. In sixth grade, we had the choice to

either keep going with Spanish—everyone at St. Chris's takes Spanish from third to fifth grade—or give French or German a try. I went for French, mostly because I'd just started listening to M83, a French band, which I admit is a lame reason to study a language.

Now I have a better one.

"Haiti was colonized by the French, but I think most of the people there speak Kreyol," Nomura says. I have no idea what *Kreyol* is, or how Nomura can know such a thing, but I try to memorize the word so I can look it up later. "The educated people probably speak both."

"So, Bijou must speak both," I say. "I mean, she goes to St. Cat's. That's educated, right?"

"She's in seventh grade," Ira says. "Is seventh grade 'educated'?"

"You guys are in seventh grade," Nomura says. "Are *you* educated?"

Rocky Van Sant struts over to us, Trevor Zelo lazing behind him as usual. Rocky and Trevor are the most popular guys in our class. By "most popular" I don't mean that any of us actually like them, of course; they're rude and obnoxious, and they spend most of their lives thinking up ways to make themselves look smarter than we are. But they're going out with Jenna Minaya and Angela Gudrun, the two best-looking and most popular seventh graders at St. Cat's. And Angela and Jenna are so good-looking that having them as girlfriends makes Trevor and Rocky, whether popular or not in the strict definition of the term, almost godlike. They are set for life—or at least until Angela and Jenna decide to dump them—and in the meantime, the rest of us are supposed to do whatever Rocky and Trevor tell us.

"Howdy, boys," Rocky smirks, leaning on our table. "What are we up to?" He doesn't actually care; he's looking for something to make fun of, which usually doesn't take him very long.

"Working on a report," I say, not wanting to give anything away.

"Oh yeah?" Trevor asks, pretending to be interested. "What's it on?"

"Haiti," I say, figuring I might as well come out with it, since Rocky's already leaning over and peering at the encyclopedia entry.

"Mr. Miller?" Rocky asks.

"Yeah," I say. "We had to pick a Third World country." I hope he doesn't ask me what the "Third World" is, because I haven't a clue.

"What do you care about the West Indies?" Rocky says. Did I mention that Rocky's the smart one? Trevor's really good-looking, with sort of caramel-blond hair and green eyes, so it's obvious why the girls like him. But Rocky, who's on the short side and twists his black hair into greasy spikes with hair gel, isn't handsome at all. He uses that evil brain of his to *trick* girls into liking him—at least, that's the only explanation I've been able to come up with.

"I didn't say the West Indies," I say. "I said Haiti."

Rocky chuckles. "Alex, life is a race, and you're so far behind, you think you're in first place."

"Nice, dude," Trevor says, slapping him a high five.

Nomura gives me one of his silent, Yoda-like "I'll explain later" looks, and I make a mental note to look up "West Indies" as soon as Rocky and Trevor are out of my sight.

"Anyway, you may have heard about the earthquake in Haiti? In 2010?" I say, busting out my facts. "That's why I chose Haiti for my report. Everybody cares about Haiti right now. How they're recovering and everything."

Rocky gives me a doubting look. "Nah, you're up to something. You're . . . breathing funny. But whatever. I'll find out soon enough."

I don't respond. Maybe if I don't say anything, he'll drop it.

"So, are you guys going to Spring Fling?" Ira asks, out of nowhere.

Trevor is taken off guard. "Jenna and Angela are going," he says. "So, yeah. Obviously." I wonder if he realizes how that sounds: like Jenna and Angela are leading the two of them around on leashes. Is that how it is, when you get the most beautiful girl? Once you've got her, you have to do whatever she says, go wherever she goes? "How about you, Ira?" he asks, looking amused.

Before Ira can answer, Rocky chimes in. "You going to bring your sister again, like at Fall Ball?"

"I didn't *bring* Maricel," Ira says. "She was just *there.* We're in the same grade."

Rocky smiles and turns toward me. "I've got an idea, Schrader. Why don't you bring *your* sister? She's gorgeous."

"Nice," Trevor says. "An older woman." They laugh and high-five again. It's a constant thing with them.

"She wouldn't even so much as look at you, Rocky," I say. "Trust me on that."

He ignores me. "Anyway, it's too bad she's not coming, because here's what's gonna happen. You guys are going to spend Spring Fling alone, just the three of you, talking about the same stuff you talk about every day at school. Only you're going to look over to the dance floor and see me and Trev dancing with the two hottest girls at St. Cat's."

"That sounds so . . . frustrating, doesn't it?" Trevor asks. "Watching other people have fun while you have the same conversation you've already had a thousand times, with the same two losers you hang out with every single day of your life?" He looks genuinely confused. "Why even bother coming at all?"

Just then, Mr. Blossom appears. Firmly placing his hands on Rocky's shoulders, he addresses all of us. "Boys, I wish you wouldn't make me say this every single Friday, but it's called a *silent* study hall for a reason. Another word out of any of you, I'll be seeing you in detention."

A smattering of *yes-sirs*, a tucking in of chairs.

Once Mr. Blossom is safely out of range, Trevor takes a seat at the next table over, checking that Blossom's back is turned before kicking his feet up and leaning back in his chair. Rocky follows him at first, but then turns back around.

"Here's what makes things tricky," he says, his voice just above a whisper. "Girls don't like scaredy-cats. If they can tell you're nervous—and believe me, they can tell—they won't come near you." He twists one of his gelled spikes, and I wonder how many times a day he has to wash that gunk off his hands. "But how can you be cool around a girl if you've never hung out with one who wasn't directly related to you? It's a genuine dilemma."

"Thanks for that pearl of wisdom," I say. However, probably the most irritating thing about Rocky is that he's usually right about this stuff.

"Look on the bright side," he says, ignoring me again. "Spring Fling's not for another twenty-four hours. Maybe you can get some, you know, experience, between now and then."

Trevor, still leaning back in his chair, says, "Schrader's definitely going to need to ditch these two if he wants a girl to take him seriously, though."

"For sure," Rocky says. "Nomura's . . . half-cool, I guess. He isn't a total disaster. But Mr. Sci-Fi over here? Total chick repellent."

I glance at Ira, who is looking over at the wall of library

books, as if scanning for a title. But I can tell he's embarrassed. And angry, although he's smart enough to know there's no way he can win here.

"Oh, and just one more word of advice, Schrader," Trevor says. "Lose the cords." He points to my fraying pants, and I can't help but take a foolish look at my own lap.

"Cords are not cool, little man," Rocky says. "Not cool at all. Even the nastiest chick at St. Cat's wouldn't go near a guy wearing those things."

"We'll see, Rocky. We'll see."

I ignore the "little man" comment—Rocky's two inches shorter than me, and he somehow thinks that calling me little will make it so—but I can't help it; once he's turned his back to us, I run my hand over my cords, wishing that I at least had something decent to wear. Knowing how to dress is way more challenging for those of us who have had no say whatsoever in what we wear five days a week, for the last eight years of our lives. But somehow Rocky and Trevor are able to figure out what's cool and what's not, and I've still got some time to do the same myself.

As for getting any "experience" in a single day, that's not going to happen. I've got to concentrate on things I can control, like learning more about Haiti, learning more about Bijou, and figuring out what the heck to wear.

5

What's Wrong With All-Boys Schools, Pt. 2

The uniform. It's got to go.

Not only are we locked away from girls from 8 a.m. to 3 p.m. every day, but we have to wear uniforms that make us look like a bunch of rich nerds. And I don't mean we have a simple dress code. I mean the same, exact uniform, every day of the week, every week of the year: navy-blue tie with red-and-gold crest design; light-blue oxford shirt; gray pants (these can be slacks or corduroys—wahoo, a huge difference!); navy blazer; black shoes (oxfords or penny loafers—you make the call!); and dress socks, also black (black socks—hot!). If I'm feeling really crazy, I wear black athletic socks, but if wearing socks that are one millimeter thicker than dress socks makes me feel like some kind of rebel, I'm in serious trouble.

And believe me, no girl who goes to a regular school is

ever going to look at a kid in a St. Chris's uniform and say to herself, *That's the one I want*—him, *the one with the gold-buttoned blue blazer and the black penny loafers!* Public-school girls think we're either dorks or wealthy snobs, and believe me, I'm not rich at all. I'm on a scholarship, and my mom can still barely pay the tuition for me and my sister, Dolly, who's a sophomore at St. Cat's High School.

I keep telling my mom that Dolly and I would be happy to go to public school. We could all split the money, I say, and hang out on the beach in Puerto Rico for a whole year. Or buy a vintage Mustang. Or go to Foxwoods Casino and gamble on a rapper's budget. Or buy a boat and sail to Puerto Rico.

There are a million things we could do with that money. I wish we could just spend it; it would be awesome!

.....ꙭꙭꙭꙭ.....

Last September, the week before school started, my mom took me shopping for school clothes, ultimately buying me three pairs of pants and four shirts. Like every year since kindergarten, I was supposed to make it until summer vacation wearing the same three versions of my uniform every day. But how do you do that without totally destroying your clothes before June? It's a major challenge.

Mom took me to H&M, which is slightly cooler than the

Gap, at least. The store had blue oxford-type shirts that fit me perfectly, loads of black dress socks—supercheap—and the gray cords that I thought would be a cool change from the *trousers* (my mom's word, not mine) I always wore.

The best thing about H&M is that the girls who work at the cash register are almost always really pretty. And that day was no different. We stood in one long line, waiting to be called by one of the three register girls, and they were all supercute and well dressed. One was white, one was black, and one was Asian. This is why New York City is awesome: it's like an international convention for hot girls!

They were all way too old for me, but it was still exciting that I was about to talk to one of them. And I figured it was like practice for talking to girls my age. Why not take advantage of an opportunity, right?

So, we finally got to the front of the line, and it was like a game of roulette, trying to figure out which cute girl was going to call us up. Finally, the white girl said, "Next!" and we walked up to the register. She was a tall brunette, probably twenty-two or so, with giant blue eyes and bangs cut at a sharp diagonal. I wish my mom could have let me buy the stuff on my own, but she was the one with the debit card, so there we were, mother and son, side by side.

"You must go to Catholic school," the brunette said as she scanned the tags.

"Kind of," I said. "It's Episcopal."

"Really? You're talking to an Episcopal schoolgirl," she said. "I mean, I was. You know, when I was younger."

"Really?" I asked. "So there's life after Episcopal school? It gets better?"

"It does indeed," she said, laughing. I could tell she thought I was funny.

I blushed even more, but I didn't care. I couldn't believe I was able to carry on a conversation with a girl this cute. And even *make her laugh.*

But before I could think of anything more to say, the girl was putting the last pair of cords into the shopping bag, and my mom said, "Now, don't lose these, honey."

This time, I blushed purple. I mean, don't lose a pair of pants?! I'm in seventh grade, and she thinks I'm going to lose a pair of pants? I haven't lost an article of clothing since I was eight. To have my mom talk to me, in public, like I was still in second grade? Humiliating.

The girl gave me a pitying smile as we left the register, but I couldn't even wave good-bye. So much for "practice."

Here's another thing: I need, I desperately need, practice. Even on weekends, those amazing forty-eight-hour stretches away from St. Chris's, I'm still at a disadvantage when it comes to girls. Why?

Because I've barely ever even hung out with any. Except my mom and Dolly, and they don't count.

Girls I'm not related to, real girls, have told me I'm

pretty good-looking (actually, just one girl, who lives across the street from my aunt Liz in Denver, Colorado. But one is better than none, right?). I have brown wavy hair, blue-green eyes, and no zits. I'm five feet seven inches tall, which is pretty good for seventh grade.

But Rocky is right. I don't know how to talk to girls. In general, I consider myself a pretty good conversationalist. I might not be as well-versed in current events as some people, but I know a lot about music, baseball, and cars, and I can tell a good joke. My mom and my sister don't care about cars, and they don't even know the rules of baseball, although they both love music, and they laugh at more than 50 percent of my jokes. But do real girls like music? And would they find me funny? There's only one way to see: I've got to find a girl to talk to.

And after eight years in boys-only purgatory, I think I might have finally found one.

6

Dolly Hits the Nail on the Head

Finally at home, I run up to Dolly's room and turn on her laptop. She's not exactly in love with the fact that Mom says I can use hers "within limits," and I'm not in love with the concept of "limits," or the fact that I live in a household that can't afford two laptops, so we're even. And I know I've got at least twenty minutes before Dolly gets back from her cello lesson, so hopefully I can learn everything I need to and get out of here before my thirst for knowledge causes a war between my sister and me.

I pull out my pen and notebook and navigate to a wiki site on Haiti. I'm taking Rocky up on his advice, although not quite in the way he intended. There's no way I can turn myself into some kind of suave lover-man overnight, but I *can* become the world's—or at least St. Chris's—leading expert on Haiti before Spring Fling. And if that fails, at least I won't be as dumb as Nomura thinks I am.

According to the wiki, here are the basics:

Haiti's an island, or more accurately, half of an island called Hispaniola, with the Dominican Republic occupying the other half. And Hispaniola is only one of a whole mess of islands in the Caribbean, including Cuba, Puerto Rico, and all the other ones where instead of paying all this money to St. Cat's and St. Chris's, my mom, Dolly, and I could be partying like rock stars. I cringe as I read that these islands are called the West Indies. This means that while Haiti has nothing to do with India, Bijou is West Indian after all.

Okay, so Rocky Van Sant knows more about Bijou, or at least her culture, than I do. Maybe I *am* an ignoramus.

I do a quick scan of the stuff Haiti's best known for. Physically, it's tiny—it's about a quarter the size of New York State—but there are nearly ten million people there, and 50 percent of them are children. It's a very poor country, supposedly the poorest in all of the Americas, and a place where a lot of people die of diseases Americans don't die of, like cholera and malaria. And while Christianity is practiced by over 95 percent of the population, many people still associate Haiti with the vodou religion (complete with zombies—Ira will love this!) practiced only by a few. One thing Haitians are superproud of: they kicked out the slave owners over two hundred years ago and have been independent ever since.

Suddenly the door opens. It's Dolly, dragging her huge,

clunky cello case—it's almost as tall as she is—over the threshold of her door.

"Computer time's over, little brother," Dolly says, startling me so much that while I'm turning around, I swing my hand across her desk and knock over a cup filled with pencils and pens.

"Very graceful. Now, how about cleaning that up and then clearing out of my room?" she asks.

I shut the laptop, a little too fast. I don't want her to see what I'm reading, even though there's nothing weird or suspicious about Haiti.

"What are you up to, anyway?" she says. She tries to pry the laptop open. "Looking at naughty pictures, are we?"

"No way," I say. "I'm writing a report." I let her open it and look at the monitor.

"Alex, it's four thirty on a Friday afternoon, and Spring Fling is tomorrow night. You're trying to convince me, your older, much wiser sister, that you're actually writing a report that couldn't possibly be due until Monday morning at the earliest?"

"Well, I'm doing research." And it's true. I am.

She turns the laptop toward her; the window I was working in is still open.

"Haiti, huh?" she says. "You're writing a report on Haiti?"

"Yeah, for social studies. Mr. Miller."

She squints and makes a *hrmph* noise. "Are you sure you're not reading about Haiti so you can impress that new girl at St. Cat's, what's-her-name?"

Who told her? And if she knows, how many other people do, too? I feel my entire face turning a dark, burning red. I cradle my cheeks in my hands to keep her from seeing, but it's pointless. "Bijou," I say, totally busted. "Her name is Bijou."

"Oh my God, that was a wild guess, but I totally hit the nail on the head, didn't I?"

I don't bother responding, but she can tell. Like Rocky said, girls can always tell.

Dolly is thrilled. "You have a crush!" she squeals. "It's totally adorable." Disgustingly, she hugs me.

"Don't tell Mom, okay?"

"Okay, okay." She lets me go, puts her cello against the wall, and sits on the edge of her bed. "Alex, that's so sweet. With everything she's been through, maybe a nice boy like you is exactly what she needs."

"What do you mean, 'everything she's been through'?" I ask. "Do you know anything? I mean, specifically?"

"Well, no, but she must have been through a lot. I mean, she lived there. She survived it. I'm sure anybody who did has a major story to tell."

"Do you think her whole family really died?"

"I have no idea. Where'd you hear that?"

"Just around." The truth is, Ira had told me, although he couldn't verify it, and neither could Maricel. Could it possibly be true, though? Losing your whole family is way too much to handle without getting put into a mental hospital or something. And Bijou definitely didn't look like somebody who needed to be locked away. I'd only seen her the one time, drinking a ginger ale at Peas n' Pickles. But to me, beautiful or not, she didn't look like some battle-scarred victim. She looked like a regular seventh-grade girl. She looked strong, not scarred or even scared.

"Well, there are bound to be rumors, but I wouldn't believe anything that doesn't come directly from her. Not that you should go up and ask her those kinds of questions. You should definitely hold off on that. Just let her share whatever she wants to share, whenever she wants to share it."

"God, I'm not that stupid. I wouldn't do that."

Dolly gives me a goofy look, puts her hand on my shoulder, and gives it a shake. "Alex, it's so sweet that you like her."

"Please don't tell Mom. I can't deal with that right now. She's so . . . cheesy about stuff like this."

"Okay. Won't say a word." She brushes her hair back behind her ear. "Promise."

7

Zip Your Fly

I don't need an alarm clock. I've got Dolly's cello.

Every weekday, my sister is up, out of bed, and starting in on a half hour of practice by 7:15 a.m. On Saturdays, she waits until eight thirty, which my mom seems to think I should consider a major blessing.

People believe the cello to be this soothing, mellow instrument, but if you live underneath one, you won't think of it that way first thing on a Saturday morning. You'll think some insane doom-metal band has suddenly arrived to play a concert right in your house. Dolly's room is in the attic, directly above mine, and I can hear the cello vibrations shake her wooden floor, inches from my ceiling, as soon as the bow hits the strings. Plus, there's a vent that runs between our rooms. I can even hear her breathing. It's horrible.

I've been complaining to my mom for two years, but she says that with Dolly's mountains of homework, morning's the only time she can practice. Dolly practices two hours a day, manages straight As, and is going for a scholarship at Juilliard, while I've got almost no musical talent, and a B is cause for major celebration. So I can complain all day, but my sister's going to play whatever she wants, whenever she wants. This morning, it's Bach's Cello Suite no. 1, which I've heard approximately sixteen thousand times.

Since I'm obviously not getting any more sleep this morning, I decide to give Dolly a hand by helping her keep the beat. It seems like a fair trade-off to me; if I have to wake up before the sun does, I should at least be allowed some entertainment. I pick up my basketball from the floor and start bouncing it against the ceiling in time to the Bach. After ten seconds, Dolly's glorious music comes to an abrupt halt, and the basketball takes a solo.

"Alex, come on," she says, her volume no louder than if I were sitting right next to her. "It's not like I want to practice. I *need* to. I've got a recital coming up in three weeks."

"I'm trying to help you, Doll," I say between basketball bounces. "You were slowing down in that one section, so I thought I could be like . . . what do you call it? A metronome!"

"Fine, I guess I'll stop for a while and go eat breakfast with Mom. There's all kinds of stuff we need to catch up on. Your new love interest, for example."

I stop bouncing the ball, and she laughs. "Forgot about that, didn't you?" she calls out before starting to play again.

It's probably for the best. I've got a dance to get ready for, and it starts in just ten hours. I've got to study up on some French vocabulary, and I've got to put my outfit together.

Girls think that guys don't stress out about what they wear. I can't speak for all of guykind, but for us Episcopal schoolboys, who spend roughly 70 percent of the week (that's five days) in uniform, getting dressed for a dance is a big deal, and there's nothing easy about it. We might not want to admit it, but it's true.

Three hours later, Nomura calls and informs me he's wearing what I call his "second uniform," the outfit he has on 99 percent of the time he's not in school: white button-down shirt, khaki pants, brown dress shoes instead of black. I've given Nomura solid wardrobe advice before, but he ignores it; he *wants* to look like the captain of some debate team. He even claims it's an intentional strategy to find a real, genuine person, not just a pretty face; if a girl can't see past his clothes, he says, nothing good will happen between them anyway, so why bother spending money on trendy clothes that will be out of fashion in six months?

"I'm wearing black DKNY jeans, light-blue polo shirt, black Converse," I say.

"No jeans at Spring Fling," Nomura reminds me.

"You don't think I can get away with black ones? You have to look pretty close to even tell they're jeans."

"Why risk it? Remember Fall Ball? Chris Donatello was kicked out for wearing jeans. No questions asked. You don't want that."

"Christianity makes no sense. I mean, Jesus walked around barefoot all day, and I can't even wear jeans to a dance?"

"Put on some black dress pants and get over yourself."

"Yeah, yeah."

"So, do you have a game plan yet?"

"Just what we talked about. The cards."

"Excellent. I think it can work." I notice that he says "can," not "will," work, but I let it go.

"Thanks. I'm on it. But did Ira do his part?"

"Relax. The deed is done."

"Sweet." Okay, I'm really, really starting to get nervous. I try to remember what Rocky said about staying relaxed. But can I pull it off?

"Oh, and last but not least: zip your fly!"

The zipper reference is no joke. Last October, during Fall Ball (my first St. Cat's dance *ever*), I went to the bathroom and must have forgotten to zip up afterward. Totally clueless, I had my fly down for at least five songs. Nobody noticed until Jenna Minaya pointed at me and yelled, "I see London, I see France" from across the gym. Angela Gudrun and a bunch of other girls burst into an endless fit of laughter. Needless to say, it was the end of my evening;

I mean, how could I ask a girl to dance after exposing my shorts in public?

But Nomura isn't just literally reminding me to zip up. He's also warning me that, as much as the dances fill our heads with a thousand images of our future girlfriends, there are risks involved, too. By talking to Bijou, I could either succeed in presenting myself as somebody she might actually find interesting, or I could ruin my chances of ever getting another St. Cat's girl to so much as look at me.

Dances are dangerous.

8

Spring Fling

It's seven fifteen, and Ira, Nomura, and I are hovering around a bowl of lime-green punch. It's like Rocky predicted—I haven't talked to anybody but my two best friends for the forty-five minutes I've been at St. Cathopher's Spring Fling. But it's early yet, and I'm still optimistic. Tonight just might be my night.

The punch doesn't taste like lime; it doesn't taste like anything at all, but it's so sweet that undissolved sugar crystals coat my tongue. After each sip, I swish the liquid around in my mouth, not letting it settle too long; I don't want my tongue to be the color of a shamrock when I finally get my chance to talk to Bijou. She'll think she's getting hit on by a leprechaun.

I'm starting to get jumpy. The DJ is playing "Umbrella," "Rock Your Body," and other oldies-but-baddies guaranteed to keep us—well, me, anyway—off the dance floor, so there's nothing to do but stand around and wait. Every single guy in our class is here except for Rocky and Trevor, but the boy-girl ratio is way out of whack. At least half the St. Cat's girls aren't here yet, and the ones who are, huddled in a corner by the bleachers at the far end of the gym, aren't the cool, popular ones. They're the shy, superawkward girls, like Elana Brooks and Meredith Chan, who can't even make eye contact without erupting into fits of giggles. Nomura, Ira, and I stay far enough away that eye contact, especially in this room's dim lighting, isn't even a possibility.

Bijou, of course, is the only girl I care about seeing, but she's not here yet. Somehow I think I'd *feel* whether she'd arrived already without even laying eyes on her, but believe me, I didn't leave it up to my sixth sense. The first thing I did when we got here was circle the entire perimeter of the gym, and I've had my eyes locked on the only entrance ever since. Bijou is not here.

"Maricel definitely talked to her?" I ask Ira. I look down and see that I'm wringing my hands, so I give them one good shake and put them in my pockets, where nobody can see them. "You're sure?"

"How many times can I say it? Mari did the job. I promise."

"But what did she say?"

"Look, I didn't follow her around and listen in on their private conversation, but I'm sure she told Bijou exactly what you guys told me to tell her to say."

I turn to Nomura. "Are you sure this is a good plan?"

"Yes," he says. "As good as we can come up with, anyway."

"It seemed good when you suggested it. But now it sounds pathetic and desperate."

"Or just plain *direct*, maybe?" Nomura says. "You need to chill, man. You're making me nervous, and I don't even have anything at stake here."

"Okay, sorry."

"And . . . you're welcome for helping you."

"Sorry . . . thanks to both of you for helping me out. I couldn't have done it without you."

"You haven't done anything yet," Ira reminds me.

"Right," I say sarcastically. "Thanks for your support."

"You bring the cards?" Nomura asks.

I pat my right front pocket. "Got 'em," I say.

He nods in approval.

Some of the other guys are shoving and horsing around with one another, trying to create a spectacle. We pay as little attention to them as possible, sidestepping them when they get too close. They're a nuisance, like mosquitoes, but not a threat. Hands in pockets, we bide our time.

Ira tells Nomura and me about *Rise Again*, a movie about

a female Iraq War veteran who saves the world from an army of flesh-eating zombies. Nomura and I nod, pretending to follow the absurdly complicated synopsis, but Ira makes no sense whatsoever. He couldn't care less that there are a dozen girls in the room, and twenty more on the way; he's as into the Syfy Channel as he was when we were eleven.

Then the doors swing open.

"Dude!" Nomura whispers, punching me in the bicep. "They're here."

I turn around to see Rocky and Trevor overlooking the dance from the threshold like little lords. "Ick," I say to Nomura. "Who cares about them?"

"Not those idiots. Look behind them."

My heart leaps as I see Mary Agnes, Maricel, and, last but definitely not least, Bijou sidestep Rocky and Trevor to circle the edges of the room. Mary Agnes is a couple of strides in front, pointing up to the streamers and other decorations along the walls, the balloons floating toward the ceiling. Maricel looks up, politely admiring, but Bijou is checking out all the kids clustered to the right of the DJ. It's her first dance, in America at least, so maybe she's nervous (although there's no way she's as edgy as I am, is there?). I pat my pocket again, checking for the tenth time that the index cards are still there, and amazingly enough, they haven't disappeared since Nomura asked about them three minutes ago.

Mary Agnes, Maricel, and Bijou have put their coats down near where the dorky girls are sitting. Mary Agnes waves at a couple of them and seems to still be pointing out the finer elements of the decor. She's probably running the dance committee single-handedly; that'd be her style.

I notice for the first time that Bijou is at least two inches taller than any other girl in the room. God, I hope she's not wearing heels. That would probably make her taller than me.

Suddenly, a tap on my shoulder. When I see Trevor and Rocky, who even by his standards has a scary amount of product in his hair, my stomach churns. These two are the last thing I need to deal with right now. Even worse, Rocky points in Bijou's direction.

"You weren't writing any report, were you, Schrader?" he says. "You were studying up on that extremely cute new girl. What's her name again?"

"Bijou," says Trevor. Ick. I hate to hear her pretty name come out of Trevor's greasy mouth. *I saw her first*, I want to say. But don't, of course.

"I like it," says Rocky. "Very French-sounding."

Did Maricel tell Jenna or Angela, and one of them told Rocky or Trevor? Or did Rocky simply hear that Bijou is Haitian and put two and two together? Either way, I'm screwed now. Rocky's bound to sabotage me; it's his favorite extracurricular activity. He really excels at it.

"I give you props for trying to do some research on her. It's a smart move, seriously," he says. "But I think you might have picked the wrong letter in that encyclopedia. You don't want 'H.' You want 'V.' For 'vodou.'"

"What?" I say, bracing for an argument. One I'll probably lose.

"Breathe, Alex, breathe." Rocky laughs. "Don't have a fit. You're so nervous all the time. Just chill."

The fact that he's right makes him that much more annoying. Every time I get into one of these face-offs with Rocky, my heart goes a million miles an hour and I have to breathe through my mouth not to show it (which probably makes me look like the biggest nerd on the planet).

"Dolls, zombies, animal sacrifices—that's creepy stuff," Trevor says. "You'd better watch yourself, Schrader. If you make her mad, she could put a curse on you and mess you up bad."

"Thanks," I say. "I'll try to keep that in mind." Of course, I've seen the same dumb horror movies on cable that everyone else has. I've seen old witch ladies drive pins into the soft fabric of a doll's heart; I've seen their victims clutching at their chests and falling dead to the floor. But just because Bijou's Haitian doesn't mean she's into that spooky stuff.

Rocky jabs Trevor and nods in my direction. "Look at Schrader, trying to figure it all out. Taxing that tiny brain of his to come up with all the answers. But he's in way over his head."

"So when it comes to girls, you two have all the answers, right?" I ask. I want it to come out edgy and sarcastic, but instead it actually sounds like a sincere question. I need to improve at this face-off stuff.

"Not answers, Alex. Questions," Rocky says. "Like, how is a geek like you ever going to have a girlfriend at all, much less a gorgeous girl like that? I mean, she's frickin' hot. That, my friend, is an unsolvable mystery."

"Maybe I'll just be myself, and you guys will keep being *your*selves," I say, calmer now. "And eventually Bijou will see that I'm a nice, normal guy, right about the same time that Angela and Jenna figure out that the two of you are complete losers."

For a second, Trevor looks almost impressed that I'm capable of talking back to them without tripping over my own words. But then he looks me up and down and says, "Alex, are those pants *pleated*? You are rocking it old-school tonight, grandpa. You should have stuck with the cords."

"Nice one," Rocky tells his friend. "But cords or pleats aren't going to make a difference, are they? The bottom line is, the two of us own this school. Every girl here wants to be with us; every guy here wants to be us. And that's never gonna change."

"Amen to that!" Trevor says.

Suddenly, there's an enormous pounding on the doors, like a small bomb exploding. We all turn to look as Angela Gudrun and Jenna Minaya stumble into the gym, cackling like maniacs. Angela and Jenna aren't only the most popular girls in St. Cat's seventh grade, they're also the loudest. Never satisfied with simply walking into a room where every guy would be instantly staring at them anyway, they have to scream, slam doors, stamp their feet.

"Speak of the devil," Rocky says. "Or devils, I should say. *Our* devils." He slaps Trevor's bicep with the back of his hand. "That's our cue, man."

Rocky jogs off without giving us another look, like a puppy whose owner has given him a swift jerk of the leash.

"Slow down, fool." Trevor smirks, and follows his friend, but slowly. "Boys run. Men walk."

No more than fifteen seconds after they've left, I look up to see Mary Agnes headed straight for the punch bowl.

This is exactly what I want, right? Mary Agnes is laser-locked on us, with Bijou and Maricel right behind her. I suddenly wish I had a few more minutes to prepare, or maybe run and hide. No such luck. Mary Agnes trots up, gives the three of us a brisk nod, then picks up the ladle and pours two cups of the syrupy liquid for Bijou and Maricel before serving one for herself. Bijou eyes it suspiciously and then takes a cautious sip.

"Hi, Alex," Mary Agnes says, looking directly at me. She's right down to business, her eyes burning with purpose. Definitely not subtle, but I've known Mary Agnes since kindergarten, and "subtle" is not a word in her vocabulary.

When Mary Agnes decides she's going to do something—whether it's running for student council (she's been class president for three years running), organizing a bake sale to benefit the homeless, or in this case, playing matchmaker with a girl she's known for about five minutes—she just rolls up her sleeves and does it. Mostly, the girl scares me. She's a little intense. But now, her aggressive approach to life stands to benefit me (I hope so, anyway), so I suppose I shouldn't be too critical.

"Hey, Mary Agnes," I say. "Hi, Maricel." I don't know whether to shake hands, or hug, or what. I wind up waving, which feels weird, since the three of them are no more than three feet away from us.

"And this"—does Mary Agnes pause for a split second here, drawing the moment out, or am I crazy?—"is Bijou Doucet."

I repeat it silently to myself, trying to memorize the name. *Doucet, Doucet, Doucet.*

"Do you want to maybe . . . introduce Bijou to your friends?" Mary Agnes asks.

"Sure. Of course." Wow, am I screwing this up already?

Everything is moving too fast. I turn to Bijou. "This is John Nomura. And this is Ira."

"That's my brother." Maricel nods toward Ira, who has pulled out his video cam. "Try to ignore him."

"Put that thing away," I order, a little too forcefully. It hadn't occurred to me to ask Ira not to film the evening's events.

"What?" he asks. "This is good stuff. We're making memories."

"Not appropriate, Ira," Maricel says. "Come on."

Finally, Ira, shaking his head, turns off the camera and puts it in his pocket.

"Anyway, good to see you, boys," Mary Agnes says. I half expect her to start shaking hands with everyone in sight. She's a little too formal, maybe, but I wish I were as sure of myself as she is. It's like she's never had a doubt or a second thought in her entire life.

Mary Agnes and Maricel are wearing almost identical outfits: skirts of different colors yet the exact same style and length, white T-shirts, and bracelets from their fore-arms to their wrists. But Bijou is wearing a full-on dress, very girlie; she's the only girl in the entire room, in fact, who's wearing one. It's blue with white polka dots, ends a little below the knees, and isn't even remotely trendy. But she could be wearing a brown paper bag and still look amazing. I make eye contact with her, say hi, and smile, but not for too long. I don't want her to think I'm weird. Or that I'm *too* into her. Bijou's got on the same patent-leather shoes as before, shiny as glass, and black tights.

"Hello," Bijou says, although her accent makes it sound more like "hallo." *Very French-sounding*, I hear Rocky echo in my head. Her voice is lower than I would have thought, but in a good way: throaty and velvety.

Mary Agnes is paying close attention, silently cheering us on, maybe, but I can't tell who knows what. Does *Bijou* know I'm into her? Does Mary Agnes? They came right up to us, which means they must know *something*. But whatever knowledge they have isn't driving them away; it's bringing them closer. For now, anyway.

I'm in a daze, unsure of what to do next, and everything is out of focus, blurry. I have my cards ready, but I can't bring them out into the open. Not now.

No one has said anything for ten or fifteen seconds, which seems a lot longer when you're surrounded by girls waiting for you to talk. I wish Nomura would somehow rescue us, but Ira beats him to it, which means that instead of a life preserver, he might be throwing out a three-hundred-pound barbell.

"Have you guys seen *Rise Again*?" he asks.

"What's that?" Mary Agnes asks.

"It's a movie," Ira says.

Why is he bringing up, of all things, a zombie movie, in front of a Haitian girl?

"Ah," says Mary Agnes, giving Ira a pitying look. "Haven't seen it."

"Enough, already. You've been talking about it nonstop for the last forty-eight hours," Maricel says.

"Because it *rocks*," Ira says.

"Zombies." Mary Agnes shrugs. "They never do anything. They just walk around grunting. Where's the drama?"

"You wouldn't say that if you'd actually seen *Rise Again*."

"Ira, *they're* interested," I say, pointing to the dork area. "Go tell the geeks about it. You can film their reactions."

Ira's mouth hangs open, like he's five years old and I've stolen his ice-cream cone. "Relax, Ira, I was only kidding," I say.

I meant it as a joke; maybe it didn't quite come out that way?

I turn to Bijou. "You look . . . very nice," I say. It's the only thing I can think of.

"All of us?" Mary Agnes asks, the hint of a smile on her lips. "Or just Bijou?"

I feel a glow of warmth spread out across my face. Can they see I'm blushing like a tomato, or is it dark enough in here for me to hide it?

"All of you," I say. "You all look really nice."

"Thank you," Bijou says, but she's not really smiling. She turns and looks toward the dance floor, where Rocky,

Trevor, Angela, and Jenna are prancing around, fully pleased with themselves.

"Great," says Maricel.

"I was hoping they wouldn't show," says Mary Agnes, shaking her head at the two most popular girls in her class.

Did I say "most popular" again? Just like with Rocky and Trevor, "most feared/despised" is more like it. But if anything, they play it bigger and bolder than their boyfriends. Angela has on heels that make her tower over almost every guy in the room, and Jenna's wearing a black skirt three inches above the knee, and she's dyed her bangs an outrageous electric blue. Angela and Jenna already have Rocky and Trevor, so they haven't come to the dance to meet guys. They're here to do what Angela and Jenna do best, which is to suck up all the attention in the room.

And it's working: we're all staring at them. Angela and Jenna, ignoring their boyfriends, have gone to the dance floor alone and are currently gyrating to Usher's "Hot Tottie." I see Mr. Price, one of the dance chaperones, on the other side of the gym. He's noticing the two crazy-hot girls dancing provocatively close to each other—you'd have to be blind to miss it—and probably trying to figure out whether, and how, to stop them. Rocky and Trevor have joined them now, but the girls are still dancing more with each other than with the guys, leaving the two boys looking awkward and out of place. I notice with pleasure that Rocky doesn't look too relaxed himself right now.

"I'm sorry," Mary Agnes says, folding her arms across her chest and aiming a death stare at the dance floor. "I don't see what's so great about them."

"Jenna's extremely, extremely attractive," Ira says. "They both are."

"Gross, Ira," Maricel says, shaking her head at her brother.

"Well, she is," Ira says.

Oh, Ira. I mean, of course Angela and Jenna are both ridiculously cute. Angela is blond, with perfect porcelain skin, and Jenna, Dominican with a deep tan that offsets her green-gold eyes, may be even prettier. But you don't share that information with other girls! That's just common sense, isn't it?

"She's good-looking, yeah, but she and Angela are totally evil. I mean, really, really cruel, for real," Maricel says. "Doesn't that count for anything?"

"Of course," I say. "If Angela and Jenna are anything like their boyfriends, I wouldn't go near them."

"That's not what you said about Angela the other—" Ira said.

Nomura cuts him off, thankfully. "I'd go near Jenna Minaya, but only if she asked me really, really nicely."

"As much as we hate them, they did get people out onto

the dance floor," Maricel says. "At Fall Ball, we all kind of stood around and stared at each other." It's true— Angela and Jenna have made it instantly cool to head to the dance floor. Ninety seconds ago it was empty, and now it's half-full.

"Well, I say if you can't beat 'em, join 'em," says Mary Agnes. "Anybody want to dance?"

"I'm in," says Nomura. Then he looks toward Maricel. "You?"

Maricel's looking cute. Golden-brown skin. Black hair cut into a bob. Does Nomura like *Ira's sister*, or is he being an awesome wingman? Mary Agnes takes a big breath, as if about to jump off a steep cliff, and asks Ira if he wants to dance, too.

"Yeah, right," Ira says.

"Ira . . . ," I whisper. "Be *cool*."

He looks confused, but he eventually follows Nomura to the dance floor. He hasn't waited for Mary Agnes, though, and as he passes her, he almost knocks her over.

I'm about to follow, too, until Mary Agnes whispers, "I'm doing this for you, you know. Stay here. Don't dance, *talk*."

Bijou and I watch them move onto the floor, now almost completely full. I smile at her, and she smiles back. But we're not talking yet, and the idea, the horrible thought that occurs to me, is that we might never talk, that I might stand here twiddling my thumbs for the rest of the dance out of pure, animal fear while this beautiful girl stands awkwardly next to me, hoping that she could talk to someone cooler, someone who at least has a clue.

So I take a deep breath, pull out my cards, and go for it.

No Boyfriends

If I had known, for even one moment, that the only reason Mary Agnes and Maricel have been pushing me so hard to come to this silly dance is to meet a *boy*, I never would have agreed to it in the first place.

I, Bijou Doucet, do not want a boyfriend.

Maman would kill me if I even smiled at a boy who wasn't an immediate member of my family (and I might even get slapped on the wrist if he *was*). She may be far away now, but she would know—she really would. And she would fly here like an angry spirit to set me straight.

Where I come from, this is the way things are: Girls go to school, then we go straight home. We go to church with our families on Sundays, then we come straight home. We help our mothers and sisters and aunts buy the food at the market, then we come straight home.

Port-au-Prince priests speak of miracles, but for me, the real miracle would be to spend five minutes without an adult carefully watching every single thing I do.

Even now, at this dance, teachers hide in the darkness on the edges of the gymnasium and observe us, making sure that no one does anything bad or wrong. Mary Agnes, Maricel, and the others pretend, because we are in school while it is dark outside and because there is a DJ spinning Top 40 music in the same room where we play each other in basketball, that we are free here. But I know the truth: the adults are watching us, all the time, and we do only what they allow us to do.

Even while I was getting dressed, my *tante*, Marie Claire, refused to let me wear the outfit I chose: my nicest jeans, white flats, and a pretty lavender top, which was a Christmas gift from Maman.

"But it's too small for you," Marie Claire said, smiling at me in that way that makes me wonder whether she truly cares for me or just feels sorry for me because I am so far away from home. "And it looks a little bit . . . old."

"This dress looks even older. It has a *collar* on it." I do not know what American girls wear to a dance, but I know they would not wear this dress.

I could have told my aunt that the shirt was a Christmas gift from my mother, and that the soft fabric, washed so many times and left to dry on the clothesline, reminded me of her. But would it have made a difference? Marie Claire and I both knew the real reason she was making me change: Tonton Pierre, my uncle, didn't want me going to the dance at all, and if he saw me come out of my room in anything less than a dress, he would refuse all over again.

"It's very pretty," Marie Claire said. Her eyes looked tired and heavy. She wanted to be done with this and see me on my way without any further argument. It had taken her forty minutes to convince Tonton Pierre, who has lived in America for almost thirty years but has never had any children of his own, that a dance is a perfectly acceptable activity for a young person here. "The child is only trying to fit in," Marie Claire had said in a voice barely above a whisper. The teachers at St. Catherine's and St. Christopher's would not allow their students to run wild in the streets, she explained. And, she hinted, the entire world would not crumble to pieces if Tonton Pierre let me out of his sight for three hours on a Saturday evening.

My aunt had worked hard, I knew, to give me the chance to spend time with my new friends, and I wasn't ungrateful.

She touched my cheek, gave me a sad smile, and said, "You said you wanted to go to this dance, and you know your uncle well enough to know that would come with certain . . . requirements."

"I know." I look up at her and try to smile.

"So, what's the matter?"

"I do want to go. Everyone is going, so why shouldn't I? But—" I shiver, even though it is not cold in this room.

"You wish your maman were here?"

"*Oui, c'est ça.*" *Yes, that's it.*

Marie Claire pulls me in to hug me. "Ah, *mon enfant.* One day, you will be together again. *Je te promets.*" *I promise.*

"All right, *tante.* I will wear it," I said. Even though I hate polka dots. She kissed me on the top of the head and pulled me into her chest again. Her shirt smelled machine-washed.

———————— ✤ ————————

"So, do you remember that boy from Peas n' Pickles?" Mary Agnes asks me as we put our coats on the bleacher seats, where only yesterday morning we sat for Friday assembly. She waves to someone, but there are flashing lights coming from the stage, where the DJ plays, so my eyes have not adjusted yet and I still can't see a thing.

"The one who was looking at his shoes?" I ask. There were two: the Japanese boy with the big, round glasses, and the white boy who was so shy he couldn't look me in the eye.

Mary Agnes raises her eyebrow. "Yes, that one. He's cute, right?"

"How would I know? I never saw his face."

Now Maricel is laughing, too. "Well, you can get a better look tonight. He's staring laser beams at us right now." She nods to her right.

I look across the gym, and even though it's still quite difficult to see, I can tell that there are three boys looking right at us. One is the Japanese boy; another is the little one, Maricel's brother. So the third must be this "cute" one. As soon as they see me returning their stare, all three quickly turn away and pretend to be in the middle of a very funny conversation.

"What was his name?" I ask. Ashley? Andrew? A typical American boy with a typical American name. I have not thought of him once since seeing him.

"Alex," Maricel says.

"He likes you," Mary Agnes says. "He's a little shy, but he's really nice."

"Wait, why are we talking about—"

"He and my brother and Nomura have been best friends since practically kindergarten," Maricel says.

"Why is he looking over here?" I ask.

Mary Agnes gives me a funny look, as if I should already know the answer. "Because he wants to . . . get to know you better," Mary Agnes says.

"Alex is sweet," Maricel says.

"Beautiful eyes," says Mary Agnes.

"Kind of a blue-green," Maricel says. "Really pretty."

"I don't want to meet him, if that is what this is about. That wouldn't—"

"Let's just go talk to them," Mary Agnes says. "That's all we're doing. Talking. Is that illegal?"

"Nope," Maricel says, giving me a light jab in the arm. "It's totally legit. Come on, Bijou."

Before I even have time to protest, Mary Agnes and Maricel are walking across the room. I can't stay here alone; I have no choice but to follow them. What are they getting me involved in?

I, Bijou Doucet, want nothing to do with boys at all.

If Tonton Pierre finds out, he will go crazy, and I will never be allowed out of the house again.

........ₑₑₑₑ ....

The next moments are a blur. First, Mary Agnes is introducing me, my first and last name, both. Very formal-sounding. The white boy's eyes go wide, and then, like last time, he looks down to his feet.

He is not my concern, though, not for the moment. I am looking around the room to see whether or not any teachers are watching us. I don't mean to seem rude, and I try to look like I am paying attention to what the others are saying. But if the adults see me being introduced to a boy, will they tell my aunt and uncle? In my old school, the nuns would have considered reporting this information a sacred responsibility!

Soon, it gets worse. Before I know it, Mary Agnes and Maricel have left me alone with this boy, with this Alex! He is smiling at me, looking me full in the face, but saying nothing. Waiting. But for what? For me to do something? I was not the one who created this scenario; I can only assume that he and my supposed friends did. And now I must come up with things to talk about?

But finally Alex reaches into the pocket of his black pants and pulls out a short stack of index cards. He looks up at me, smiles in an embarrassed way, cheeks red like apples, and reads from the card: *"Depuis combien de temps vivez-vous aux États-Unis?"* How long have you lived in the United States?

He's speaking to me in French! But why?

"Je suis arrivée ici il y a deux mois," I say. But he doesn't seem to understand, so I translate: "I have been here since two months' time."

"C'est tout?" he asks. *Is that all?* He must know I speak English, doesn't he? How would I go to St. Catherine's if I didn't?

"Oui," I say. *"Je suis arrivé à Brooklyn un dimanche, et puis j'étais déjà à l'école dès lundi."* I arrived in Brooklyn on a Sunday and was already in school by that Monday.

I look toward the dance floor. Nomura, Maricel, and

Mary Agnes are dancing and smiling. Maricel's brother is just standing there, his hands in his pockets. But then he pulls out—what is it with these boys and their pockets?—a video camera and begins to film them. Immediately, Maricel, annoyed, swats at it. Then the brother walks away, toward the bleachers, where small groups of boys and girls talk among themselves without mixing.

Alex points to my cup of punch and asks, *"Admirez-vous votre liquide?"*

I can't help but laugh; it's funny. Do I admire my liquid? Maybe he's *trying* to make me laugh?

He turns red again, though, and says, *"Excusez-moi. Je suis désole."* *Excuse me, I'm sorry.*

I smile to let him know I am not offended, sip from my punch, and say, *"Oui, c'est assez bon."* *Yes, it's good.* Then, in English, "I should not have laughed; it's very rude. You just said, 'Do you like your *liquid*,' and it strike me as funny for a moment."

"Do you guys speak English in Haiti, too? I thought it was Kreyol and French." He looks so relieved and lets the index cards rest by his side.

"Well, not everyone speaks English, but we have a—how do you say—satellite? For television? So I watch *Sesame Street* when I was little, and I learn English from this."

"Really? You grew up watching *Sesame Street*? Me

too!" Then, one more time, he colors and looks at his shoes. "Not anymore, though. I haven't watched it for a long time." What is he embarrassed about now? Doesn't everyone here grow up watching *Sesame Street*?

"Also, my mother, she watch *Tous Mes Enfants* every day," I continue. "You know, the opera?"

He pauses for a moment, looking confused. "You mean *All My Children*?" he says. "The soap opera?"

"*Oui*, I love this. I watch with my mother at home, all the time, from the satellite. Do you like it, too?"

"Well, it's okay, I guess. It's mainly . . . for women here." Well, this is one thing that is true in both our cultures; my uncle would never watch *Enfants* unless he was forced into it by Marie Claire.

But I tease the boy anyway. "Ah, so it is not, how you say, 'cool' for you to watch it, then?"

"No, it's not that—"

"Not manly enough for a growing American boy?"

He colors again, and I feel badly. "I'm sorry. *Je rigoles.*" *I'm teasing.*

But he recovers more quickly this time. He seems to have forgotten his cards for good now. "I like the way you speak French. I like . . . the sound of it. It's cool."

"*Merci, monsieur.*" Thankfully, he gets the joke of my calling him "monsieur," and we both laugh.

"So, you had satellite TV in Haiti?" As if this is the most incredible thing he has ever heard.

"Sure, of course." He probably thinks, like most Americans, that Haiti is all shacks and tents, and people starving to death. "We had more channels in Port-au-Prince than my aunt and uncle have in Brooklyn."

"And you learned English just by watching shows?"

"Well, yes, but I also visit New York almost every summer since I was a little girl," I say. "To see my aunt and uncle. So I speak English then, also. And take some lessons for writing, too."

"Well, you speak really well," he says.

"Which you like better, my French or my English?" I don't smile; I want to see what he is going to do.

He stammers, "I . . . I . . . they're both—"

"I'm only teasing, Alex. It is a bad habit of mine. I'm sorry."

"It's okay, it means I have to stay on my toes with you."

"What does this mean, 'to stay on my toes'?"

"Oh, it just means I have to pay attention."

Ah, very true. But he might want to stay on his toes also because, while he is tall, I may even be a bit taller!

"So, is that where you live now, in Brooklyn?" he asks.

"Yes, we live in Flatbush. Many Haitians live there." I smile. "Is that one of the questions on your cards?"

"Umm, yeah, it is." He looks not so embarrassed this time. Maybe he is okay with teasing, now that he knows I mean nothing bad by it. "So, we're neighbors," he continues. "Sort of, anyway. I live in Ditmas Park."

I've never heard of this Ditmas Park, but this is only because Tonton Pierre barely lets me go anywhere but school and church. "Is that close by?"

"Yes," Alex says. "Very close."

I look around to make sure no adults are looking at us. Then I lean a tiny bit closer to him and ask, "What else is on the cards?"

"Oh, nothing. Just some . . . notes."

"Notes on what? Things to talk about with the strange new girl from Haiti?" I hold out my hand. "Show me."

"No," a girl's voice behind me says. "Show *me*."

It's Angela Gudrun, with Jenna Minaya. Two boys, a short one with dark hair, and a tall, handsome one, are standing with them.

"What?" Alex says. "No."

I really don't like these two, Angela and Jenna. On my first day at St. Catherine's, Jenna was very friendly, asking me questions about my life, my family, my friends from home. And I tried to be friendly in return. But for her, friendship meant following Angela and her around everywhere they went. And they were very rude to the other girls, making fun of them and calling them names behind their backs. I don't want this kind of person for a friend. I have kept my distance ever since.

"Come on, Schrader, what are they?" asks the short boy, taking a step forward. His hair is shiny and greasy. "Show her."

And the two boyfriends are nearly as bad, with their expensive phones and fancy clothing. They have *everything*. So why do they need to treat other people like this?

Suddenly, Nomura, Maricel, Mary Agnes, and Ira have returned. Now everyone is staring at Alex and wondering what his cards say. Why won't they mind their own business? Can't they see the cards are private to him?

"They're just notes!" Alex cries. A bit too loudly, almost yelling.

"They're jokes," Nomura says. "Alex wants to be a stand-up comic. He needs to practice."

"Come on, let's have a look," says Angela, stepping forward and ripping the cards from Alex's hand. She starts to read the cards. Alex looks like he wants to disappear.

Jenna looks me up and down. "Nice dress, Bijou," she says. "Looks about a hundred years old. Is it a hand-me-down from your grandma? Or something one of your little *friends* picked out for you?"

I see. If I am not friends with this girl, she is determined to make me an enemy. I don't bother to answer. What is the point of wasting my breath on a girl like this?

Jenna turns her attention to Angela. "Come on, Angela, what do they say?" she whines. "We're wasting our time here."

"Hold up," Angela says. "I'm enjoying this."

"All right, out with it," says the tall boy. "Read 'em, already."

Angela suddenly explodes with laughter. "No . . . way!"

"What?!" all her friends say at once, like robots.

"They're questions . . . for *her*"—she gestures toward me—"in *French*!"

"Let me see," the short boy says, and Angela hands the cards to him.

"Don't, Rocky," Alex says.

The one called Rocky puts on a French accent and screams out, "Mademoiselle, where do you *leeeve*? How long have you *beeeeen* in *les États-Unis*?"

Jenna rips the cards away from Rocky and jabs the tall boy. She is really having fun. "Check it out, Trevor: 'I hope your family is okay! I pray they did not get hurt in the earthquake!'"

I look over at Alex, who is now holding his head in his hands. Was he really going to ask me about my family? Mary Agnes and Maricel were right. This is a very sweet boy.

The tall boy, Trevor, grabs the cards. "Wait, here's the best part," he cackles. "'Do you want to go see a movie with me on Saturday?'"

"He did not actually write that out in French, did he?" Rocky says. "That's so pathetic."

"I can't believe he asked her about the earthquake," says Angela.

"I know," says Rocky. "Kid does *not* know how to talk to a girl." They all laugh.

"That's enough, guys," Mary Agnes says. "Give them back." They ignore her, though; all four of them are laughing so hard they can barely breathe.

"Wait, the queen geek is right," Rocky says, taking the cards back from Trevor. "We're being really rude. We should give these back to their rightful owner."

He holds the cards out to me. "What's your name, again?"

"Bee-something," says Jenna. "I can never remember."

"My name is Bijou," I say, loud and clear, looking dead into Jenna's eyes. What a liar she is!

"Very nice to meet you, Bijou," Rocky says, holding the cards and bowing to me as if he is a European gentleman (far, far from it). "I believe these are yours. That is, unless you want to keep reading them out loud to her, Alex?"

Alex tries to grab them from Rocky, but the greasy-haired boy easily steps to the side, holding the cards above his head.

"Oooh, feisty," Rocky says. "You must really be into this chick, huh?" Then he turns to me and says, "You know, you can do much better. Yesterday this guy didn't even know what the West Indies were. He was like, she's *Haitian*, man, not West Indian. Funny, right?"

"Shut up, Rocky!" Alex yells.

But Rocky just laughs. "I think we should give Bijou here a little present. You wrote them for *her*, after all, didn't you?" Blocking Alex with his arm, he hands the cards to me.

But Alex can't take it anymore. He twists Rocky's arm behind his back and gives the boy a hard shove. Rocky rocks back on his heels but is still standing. "Whoa, looks like I hit a nerve." He laughs, not hurt at all. "Although with Schrader, that's pretty easy to do." He turns to me again, a sneer on his lips; I wish he would stop doing this, addressing me directly as if we are having a private conversation. I would never speak privately with a person like this. "Dude is *very* touchy."

Nomura steps between us. "Rocky, why don't you guys take off." His voice is barely above a whisper, but it's sure and confident. "Come on."

Rocky considers for a moment and says, "Not that you've got any say in this, Nomura, but I think our mission's accomplished here."

The four of them walk back toward the dance floor, snickering. Rocky trips Trevor, and the girls laugh. They're on to have fun somewhere else, at someone else's expense.

But then Trevor turns around and comes up to me. "Hey, I'm sorry if we got a little carried away," he whispers. "Rocky's . . . kind of an idiot sometimes. But he didn't mean anything by it."

Jenna, on the edge of the dance floor, calls out, "Trev,

you coming or not? Mission accomplished, remember? What are you still talking to her for?"

"She doesn't want to talk to you, anyway," Mary Agnes tells him.

Everyone seems to know what I want before I even have the opportunity to open my mouth.

"Fine," Trevor tells Mary Agnes. Then to me, "I'll see you later, Bijou."

When I turn back to our group, Alex is gone.

"Where did he go?" I ask.

Nomura looks to the side and behind him. "I don't know," he says. "He . . . slipped away."

"That was so awful," says Maricel. "Why do they always have to ruin everything?"

"Come on, Ira, let's go find him," Nomura says. And the two boys jog off to look for their friend.

I see Miss Williams, our math teacher, walking in this direction. I hope she is not coming to talk to us!

Mary Agnes approaches me, takes my two hands in hers. "I'm so sorry, Bijou. I had no idea something like that would happen. I just wanted to—"

"I suppose you meant well, but don't you think it is more, how do say, courteous to talk to me before putting me in such a situation?"

Mary Agnes is apologizing, but I'm not listening. I'm looking over her shoulder, where Miss Williams is standing patiently. She waits for Mary Agnes to finish her apology and comes to stand in front of us.

"Looks as if we had a bit of drama here, didn't we, girls?" she asks, although it is clear that this is a question she does not want us to answer.

"No, ma'am," says Mary Agnes. "Just the boys being silly, is all. Nothing serious."

What she means, of course, is, nothing you need to tell our parents about.

"A tempest in a teapot, eh, Ms. Brady?"

"Yes, ma'am."

"Well, it's nice that you've taken Bijou here under your wing, but perhaps you should take a bit better care of her in the future than you did tonight."

"Yes, ma'am," Mary Agnes and I both say, although I realize the response was not mine to give.

"I wouldn't want to have to tell either of your families that there was a bit of a . . . skirmish, shall we say?" She clasps her hands together and looks down at us over the top of her glasses. "One involving a number of rather unpleasant boys?"

"No," we say in unison.

"That's what I thought." She claps her hands together, imitating joy. "Enjoy the rest of your evening, girls."

A part of me would like to tell her that I, Bijou Doucet, want nothing to do with any sort of boys at all. But another part of me would like to tell her that not *all* the boys I met tonight were so unpleasant. Alex was quite sweet and fun to talk to, and yes, he has very pretty eyes.

But of course, I say nothing of that. I say only, "Yes, ma'am."

 10

A Little Bit Cute

It's the Wednesday after the Spring Thing. Mary Agnes and I have gotten ginger ales and Utz at Peas n' Pickles, and we spread our snacks across torn paper bags on the bench seats overlooking the East River.

"Did you see the look on Jenna's face?" Mary Agnes says. "When Trevor came back with that apology, or whatever it was? I thought she was going to freak."

"Let her 'freak,'" I say. "She can't hurt me. I don't know why she has some problem with me."

"I know why. She was the prettiest girl in our class, and now you are."

"Stop." I turn my head and laugh. "I am not."

"Trevor seems to think so. And so does Alex."

"Really, Mary Agnes. Don't be ridiculous."

"Listen, before you got here, Jenna was, like, queen of

everything. She got tons of attention. Not just from boys, but from teachers, girls, everybody. But now that you're here? Maybe she's suddenly not quite so fascinating anymore."

I shrug. "I can't help it if her boyfriend talks to me. Or if Alex does."

"You don't think he's cute?" Mary Agnes asks. "Even a little bit?"

"Which one?"

Mary Agnes laughs. This is the thing I like most about her. She seems serious and bossy much of the time, but she likes to laugh, too, and she does it long and hard. "Alex," she says. "You think I want to get you thinking about Trevor? Eww. He's so conceited."

"Yes, Alex, he's cute," I say. "And he's very nice. But the point is that I cannot have a boyfriend. Ever."

"I know, I know, it's not allowed in your culture. I get that, but what does it mean? You can't even talk to a boy until you're twenty-one or something?"

I laugh. "This is how it works in a Haitian family."

"But you're in America now, not Haiti."

"That is what everyone keeps telling me: 'You're in America now.' But are things so different here? Is it so common, to see a white American boy walking down the street with a black girl? A Haitian girl?"

"Well, I don't know if it's common, exactly, but it

definitely happens. That's the way it is in the U.S. Which *is* your new home, right?"

"Haiti is my home, Mary Agnes. It will always be my home."

She bites her lip. "I'm sorry. I didn't mean to—"

"I would give anything to be home right now, in my real home, with Maman."

Mary Agnes takes my hand. "I'm sorry, Bijou, really. I didn't mean anything by it. Sometimes I forget about, I don't know, everything you must have been through."

I smile weakly and pat her hand. "It's all right. I'm just a little sensitive sometimes," I say. If she thinks she's going to make me cry like Oprah Winfrey, she can wait all day. It's not going to happen.

"You're so together, I forget. You know?"

I suppose it's better to have someone like Mary Agnes, who forgets, than all those nosy teachers at St. Catherine's, always making me look them right in the eye, asking me how I am doing, as if I am some wounded animal.

The truth is that I also forget. If I spent every moment of every day thinking about those buildings, crumbling like paper, about my neighbors dead or dying, about Maman so far away, I would go crazy. When I am with Mary Agnes, or Maricel, or even Pierre and Marie Claire, I put away that part of myself, that Port-au-Prince Bijou, like clothes in a suitcase. I shut the lid and pretend it is not there.

"Anyway, being in America, being away from my mother, is even more reason why I can't be with any boy," I say. We have finished our snacks and are now walking up Old Fulton Street, back toward school. "My uncle would be angry to know even that I am with *you* after school. If he and my aunt were not both at work all day, he would be punishing me for arriving only thirty minutes after I am supposed to."

"But that's crazy."

"To you, maybe. To me it is a little bit crazy that you get to do whatever you want. No one I knew before you and Maricel lives in this way."

"Wow."

We walk up Henry, past Cranberry Street. I wonder who named these streets. The first time I saw Pineapple Street, I looked up at the trees, hoping to see a bit of island fruit, but only the names are tropical. Everywhere in Brooklyn, it is only snow and concrete, and the coldest wind I have ever known.

"Oops!" Mary Agnes says. "Speak of the devil." She nods up the street.

A block away, he walks out of Peas n' Pickles. Not a devil, though—he, him, the boy, Alex. Before the Spring Thing, I'd only seen him once. Now, he seems to be everywhere.

"You planned this, Mary Agnes?"

"No, I didn't. Promise."

"I hope this is true." I give her the eye. "No more secret plans, please."

His other friends, the one called John and the other one, Maricel's brother, catch up to him on the sidewalk.

"God, Bijou, relax. It's Peas n' Pickles. Everybody from St. Chris's and St. Cat's goes here, almost every day. It's hardly a coincidence. We've seen Alex here before. More than once, too."

"Maybe you did, but I didn't."

"That's right, you not only never think of boys, you can't even see them with your own two eyes."

"Not until this moment did I care to, no." She looks at me, surprised, but I smile to let her know I am only joking. Mary Agnes rolls her eyes at me.

"Hi, guys," she says as we pass the boys.

"Hi," they say at exactly the same time.

"Where are you guys going?" Alex asks. Everyone here calls each other "guys," I've noticed, whether they are talking about boys or girls. A bit strange, no?

"Umm, to get snacks, obviously," says Mary Agnes. "Duh."

"That's where we're going," Alex says.

"Don't you mean that's where you just were?" asks Mary Agnes.

I almost feel bad for Alex. He was probably perfectly relaxed before he saw me, and now he's shy again.

"Okay, then, we'll see you later," Mary Agnes says. She walks away, and I follow her. I look back at the boys once. They're as frozen as sculptures. Nomura very serious, Ira looking up at the sky with his mouth wide open, and Alex looking after us with puppy eyes as if his life were crumbling all around him. If only he could see himself. So much drama, and just over a couple of girls!

"Cat got your tongue, Alex?" Mary Agnes calls over her shoulder. "I guess you really did need flash cards!" Then she starts running toward the store, taking my hand and pulling me down the street.

"Ooh, that was cruel!" I laugh once we're inside.

"Maybe." She has a mischievous look on her face; she loves this. "Anyway, I thought you wanted nothing to do with them."

"I don't, but I don't want to be mean, either."

"Oh, it wasn't so bad. I was only teasing him a little. He's crushing out on you, hard. It's pretty cute."

"But he looked so, how do you say, pitiable? All three of them did."

"We call it pathetic. Totally pathetic. Can't they think of anything to say? Can't they try to act normal and act like regular people?" But I can tell she is more amused than annoyed.

"Are all American boys like this?" I ask.

"No, there are other kinds." She makes a sour face.

"You remember those other guys from the dance, Rocky and Trevor?"

"Yes." How could I forget?

"Those are the other kind."

I'm glad, of course, that Alex isn't like Rocky and Trevor. He is better-looking and sweeter than they are, but somehow he doesn't *know* it. How is it that an uninteresting boy like Rocky can look in the mirror and see a movie star, and another, a truly handsome one like Alex, is so nervous he can barely even speak a full sentence to me without a set of cards to rely on?

"Maybe this was a good thing," I say. "I never would have said this to him, but at least now he'll stop looking at me with those sad eyes."

"Actually, after that, Alex will probably be more interested than ever."

"*Comment?* What do you mean?" I have a sip. This drink tastes nothing like ginger, but I still love it, the way the bubbles burn my throat.

"Boys want what they can't get. Or what they *think* they can't get."

I squint at her, trying to see who Mary Agnes is, *what* she is.

"Friends aren't supposed to get each other into trouble," I say. "What are you up to?"

"Maybe getting into a little trouble is exactly what you need right now."

Oh my Lord, is Mary Agnes the right friend for someone like me? "Trouble is the last thing I need in my life. You know that, right?" I say.

"Not bad trouble, Bijou. Good trouble. Just a little bit of fun. That's allowed in Haitian culture, right?"

"No, it's not!" I say, laughing. "In my uncle's house, fun is absolutely forbidden!"

Rara Surprise

Early Sunday evening, Tonton Pierre, Tante Marie Claire, and I are just finishing dinner when the doorbell rings. They don't know who it is, but I do!

Tonton Pierre shrugs and walks to the door, trying to hide a secret excitement. He thinks it is one of his old-man friends at the door, with an invitation to play backgammon or cards at the barbershop, where he is spending half his lifetime. But my uncle is about to be disappointed. Jou Jou is the one at the door, so I am the one who will be having a bit of fun tonight.

"Ah, *c'est seulement toi*," Pierre says to my brother. *It's just you.*

"*Bonjour*, Tonton Pierre," Jou Jou calls out, clutching the rada, a drum we use in Haitian music, under his arm. He doesn't try to hug my uncle—Tonton Pierre doesn't like hugs—but my brother doesn't bury his happiness, either. His eyes bounce around the room, full of energy, hungry to take in all they can, even in this room he knows so well, this kitchen where he has eaten so many meals and sat through so many of Tonton Pierre's stubborn speeches.

"Keep that bloody animal skin out of my house," Tonton Pierre says, going back to English. Tonton Pierre is always telling Jou Jou and me that we must speak "American" if we are going to get anywhere in this country, but when he's alone with Marie Claire, or with his card-playing old men, he himself speaks Kreyol.

"Yes, sir," Jou Jou says.

"Lay it on the stoop. I don't want it stinking up the room." Pierre sniffs hard. "Come on now."

"He heard you, Pierre," Marie Claire says. And it is true: since leaving this house shortly after he turned eighteen, my brother has realized that following my uncle's rules, or at least appearing to, is the best way to keep the old man quiet.

"Marie Claire, you are looking very nice tonight," Jou Jou says, kissing our aunt. From the shopping bag he pulls out two enormous mango fruits, big as melons.

"Aah, they are perfect," Marie Claire says, greedily pulling them toward her before anyone can take them away.

"You are the perfect one, Auntie," Jou Jou says, kissing

her hand like a gentleman. I roll my eyes. My brother is shameless, always flattering, like Gran-Papa, before he became so old that I was caring for him more than he was for me. Like my grandfather when he was young, Jou Jou is not stupid or unaware; it is only that he refuses to fall into the dark mood of this house. Jou Jou will not let Tonton Pierre, no matter how grumpy he is, spoil his mood.

"You come here to take our niece away from us again?" Pierre asks, as if I am not in the room. "It's very late for a school night. She must wake at seven tomorrow morning."

"I'll have her home early, Uncle, I promise you."

"The sun will be down in an hour, boy." Who else but Uncle would call Jou Jou a boy? Anyone who looks at him can tell he is a man, but Tonton Pierre needs to keep my brother in his place. "Think about what you are saying."

Jou Jou pretends to check the watch on his wrist. It's a game I've seen them play before. "You are right, Uncle," he says. "Ninety minutes, then? I can have her back by eight thirty. Is that all right?"

My brother looks at Marie Claire with his big brown eyes. He is the stray dog she cannot help but pet and love.

"Let Jou Jou be with his sister, Pierre," my aunt says. "He is good with her."

"We didn't take her off the streets of Port-au-Prince only to put her on the streets of Brooklyn," Tonton Pierre says. "We took her off her grandfather's hands because he couldn't handle the girl anymore."

"I can handle her. Right, Bijou?" Jou Jou winks at me. "At least for one evening."

"These people you go with are not good people." What my uncle means is, they are not Christian people. "They belong to no one. They belong only to the street."

Jou Jou almost responds, but he thinks better of it.

"Bijou is safe with Jou Jou," Marie Claire says. "He is her *brother*."

"Joseph, you can't possibly continue with that devil's music." Tonton Pierre is forgetting that we are talking about whether or not I can go to the park and not his favorite subject: *the sins of rara*. "Good people have no time for this street music, nephew. Which is why I'm so disappointed in you. You could have done something with your life. You still can. A doctor, a respectable businessperson, someone who would build up the community instead of hurting it. But instead of helping anyone, all you do is drive that dollar van around and play your drum until all hours of the night."

Jou Jou can't hold back anymore. "Uncle, I do help our people. I help bring our own culture back to us, here in America."

"That's not your culture, boy. You were raised right. That's some peasant culture, ignorant fools banging on drums all day because they don't know any better. Because they haven't gotten either education or the sense to follow a more righteous path."

"Uncle, at the Gran Bwa, it's not only the poorest Haitians who come out to march to the music. It's everybody, the whole community."

"It isn't anybody I know, I can assure you that."

"If you could only see the looks on everybody's face, Tonton. The joy they feel in hearing their own music, seeing they own culture, here in Brooklyn. It's magic."

"Bijou will be fine," Marie Claire says, staying calm, not looking up as she does the dishes. Safety and security are everything to my uncle. What this means for those of us living with him is that we are almost never allowed to leave our own home.

"It is a sin, I tell you." Tonton Pierre throws up his hands, but I can tell he is tiring of this argument. We have won!

Which means I get to go to Prospect Park to see the rara with my brother, while Marie Claire must stay home with my uncle, who steals all the stale air in this house with greedy lungs.

...———ℓℓℓℓ———...

The sun is out on Rogers Avenue, but there is a brisk wind that makes the hairs on my arms stand up. As Jou Jou and I walk toward the park, we pass schools, auto garages, and,

mostly, churches: the Gospel Tabernacle Church of Jesus
Christ, the New Life Center of Truth. Everything here is
new, new, new! And yet the buildings look so old and dirty.
If a church has "new" in its name, shouldn't the priests
wash it once in a while?

"How could you stand living with that man for three
entire years, Jou Jou?" I ask him.

"Tonton is not so bad, sister," Jou Jou says. "Next to
Papa, the man is a saint."

I never really knew our father; he left us when I was
very young. But from what Maman and Jou Jou tell me, I
did not miss very much. So I don't. Miss him, I mean. My
brother, mother, Gran-Papa, and Gran-Maman were
always enough of a family for me.

More churches: Dios con Nosotros Baptist Church,
Right with God Ministries. There are so many houses of
God in Flatbush, it would seem as if every person in America is in love with religion. But now we're walking by a restaurant where the smell of frying meat passes through a
steamy vent. Which do Americans love more: God or ham-
burgers? In Flatbush it is hard to tell.

"How can you say Tonton is so wonderful? You left
his house as soon as you had twenty dollars in your pocket."

"The two of us see things different, it's true." He looks
me in the eye. "But Tonton is . . . cranky. The man *means*
well."

To our right, on Snyder Avenue, is the police station. With its large facade made of brick and rough concrete, it looks like a school for bad children. To the right of the station is a painting of a policeman. GREATER LOVE HATH NO MAN THAN TO LAY DOWN HIS LIFE FOR HIS FRIENDS, read the words under his smiling face, and I suddenly realize that this policeman died, and this is his memorial. Did he really die the death of a hero, as the quote says, while trying to protect his friends?

I think of all the people *I* saw fighting and dying for the lives of family and friends. These are *my* heroes: my schoolteacher, Madame Jean-Baptiste, directing all the children out of her classroom, trying to point the way to safety with a hand that was bleeding and badly broken; our headmaster, who cried tears of joy when he saw that everyone in his school was living, only to discover after walking six miles that his own wife and young son lay dead under rubble at home; and Gran-Papa, who ran to cover Maman's body with his own as soon as he felt the house begin to shake.

"You hear the drums?" Jou Jou asks.

"Don't tell me you can hear them this far away, crazy man," I say.

"Of course I can. When you feel the drum in your spirit, the way I do, you have the senses of a superhero. A god!"

"You don't even have the sense of an animal."

"Oh, but I do, Bijou!" He jumps at me, fast as a cat, spreading his ten fingers to tickle me.

"Don't!" I cry out, laughing already. He hasn't tickled me once since I arrived here in January, because he hasn't needed to; the threat is always enough.

"Tell me you don't hear *that*," he says, cupping his hand to his ear.

"I don't hear nothing," I say.

"*Any*thing," he says. "You don't hear *any*thing." Jou Jou likes to correct my English whenever he can, but we both know I speak as well as he does. While I was learning grammar from *Tous Mes Enfants*, he was playing football— what Americans call soccer—with his friends in the field behind our house in Port-au-Prince.

Finally I do hear the thumping of the drums, the cries of the metal konets. I remember Pierre calling Jou Jou's drum a "bloody animal skin." He meant to make an insult, yes, but the sound of rara truly is a living thing: the drums like a heartbeat, the konet horns rising above the rhythm like birds taking flight.

We always thought Jou Jou would be a great football player, not a musician. But soon after he came to New York ("For a better education!" my uncle claimed), he learned to dance with his hands instead of his feet. Every week, he would call Maman and me speaking of nothing but drums, and of Rara Gran Bwa, the band he had heard playing in

Prospect Park. They were master musicians, he said, and if his dream were to come true, he would one day be asked to play the rada—a cone-shaped vodou drum with a cow-skin head—with them.

That day did come, a little over a year ago, and no sooner did Jou Jou get the invitation than he moved out of my aunt and uncle's house and into a tiny Flatbush apartment with two other members of Rara Gran Bwa. So much for Jou Jou's "better education." He is so poor now, sometimes he can barely afford to pay his rent. But I have never seen him so happy. He is living his dream.

The pounding of the drums gets louder as we twist through a small opening in the park fence along the avenue. The late-March sky is beginning to darken, and merry sounds fill the air: the chatter of Sunday picnickers, insects buzzing, little children playing their games. I love Prospect Park, the tall tree tops, the smell of leaves, the sun over the lake.

Jou Jou and I are walking along the broad path in the park, runners and cyclists whizzing by us, when I hear a voice say, "Look, it's Bijou."

Two boys on bikes stop, turn, and look at me. It's Nomura and Alex. Suddenly these two are everywhere I turn!

"Hey, Bijou," says Nomura.

And Alex manages to push out a quiet "Hiya."

In Port-au-Prince, no boy schoolmate would ever walk up to me and speak to me so boldly. But this is the United States, where there are no rules at all.

"Hello," I say.

"It's . . . nice to see you," Alex says.

A moment of quiet before Nomura says, "Did you . . . have fun at the dance?" Alex gives him a look.

"It was all right, I suppose." I stop, not sure how to continue. Did any of us have "fun" that night?

"Hi, guys. I'm Jou Jou, Bijou's older brother." The boys shake his outstretched hand. "You must forgive Bijou's silence. She used up all her words on the way over."

The boys laugh, and I glare at the idiot Jou Jou, always looking for a chance to embarrass me.

"I'm John Nomura, and this is Alex."

"You boys ridin' around the park, then?" Jou Jou asks. "Nice night for it."

I don't know whether Jou Jou is just being Jou Jou or whether my brother is trying to torture me on purpose. But either way, his friendliness makes this situation even more awkward. I suddenly wish my uncle were here; he would dismiss these boys with a wave of his hand, and they would be afraid to ever speak to me again.

"What are you guys up to?" Nomura asks. Alex looks happy that at least one of the two of them is able to speak in my presence.

"We go to the Gran Bwa, the drum circle." Jou Jou raises the rada and plays a flourish on the cow-skin drumhead with his right hand. "Can't you tell?" I try to catch my brother's eye. He is being a bit too friendly with these two. Can't *he* tell I want to make this visit we are having as brief as possible?

"Oh yeah," Nomura says. "We just passed it. Those guys are loud!"

"Not *loud*, my friend. These are master drummers playing over there." He shifts the drum from one arm to the other. "Hey, you want to join us? I promise, you will love it."

I jab Jou Jou in the ribs, but he just laughs, enjoying my discomfort. He is evil sometimes, my brother. How does he know Alex and Nomura will "love" the rara? Most Americans hate our music, call it a bunch of noise.

"I'll go!" says Alex, a bit too much excitement coming through, which, of course, makes him blush bright red, like he did at the dance.

"That's the attitude, man," says Jou Jou. "And how about you, John?"

"Actually, I'm late already. Got to get home." Nomura looks quickly to his friend, then smiles with satisfaction. "Alex, tell me all about it, cool?"

"Uh, sure," Alex says.

"Is this a good idea, Jou Jou?" I ask, hoping that there

may still be a way out of this, even if it makes me seem a bit cruel. "Will Rara Gran Bwa want outsiders to hear their rehearsal?"

"Maybe I should head back, myself," Alex says. "If it's a rehearsal."

"Sister, you well know it's no rehearsal today. Alex, come on, you going to be my personal guest. All right?"

"Okay," Alex says, smiling but still looking a little scared.

"It's settled, then," Jou Jou says, shaking Nomura's hand good-bye. I'm going to kill him later. "John, we meet again sometime soon, all right? It's always a pleasure to meet my little sister's schoolmates."

"Later," Alex says. He and my brother wave good-bye to Nomura as he rides away.

"Bye!" Nomura calls from behind his back, whizzing away toward home. I wish *I* could race home on a bike and leave my brother and the boy to become friends for life.

"All right, Alex, come with us," Jou Jou says. "You're in for a treat." He swings the rada around, playing a beat with his calloused palms. He leans over toward me and whispers, "I do this for you, Bijou. Looks like in Port-au-Prince you forgot how to make new friends." I'll get him for this when we get home.

When we arrive, we see a circle of ten or twelve men, all Haitian, in a shady grove of trees between the bike path and Parkside Avenue. About twice as many people look on, moving their bodies to the rhythm. "Hey, Jou Jou!" two or three of the musicians call out as he joins the line of three other drummers. Now I am alone with Alex, and I try to guess what he is thinking. He's probably never been to the Caribbean part of Flatbush before, and he's certainly never joined the scary Haitians beating on their animal skins in the middle of Prospect Park.

I glance at him, though, and see no fear on his face at all. Listening to the music, he looks relaxed, happy. This means, at least, that I don't have to struggle to think of things to say to him; for the moment he is absorbed by something other than me or his own embarrassment. I cross my arms and try to calm myself enough to enjoy Rara Gran Bwa, which is, after all, the reason I came here in the first place—to hear my brother play the music he loves with all his heart.

Some of the musicians are as young as Jou Jou, others as old as thirty or forty, each of them holding at least one instrument. In the center of everything is a tall, skinny man, wearing white pants with the Rara Gran Bwa logo stitched in bright yellow letters up and down the legs. The man wears a knit cap on top of a mountain of dreadlocks and rubs a small stick against what looks like a shaker of salt. He makes swift, buzzing patterns, eyes closed like he is praying.

Other men play snare and tom-tom; maracas; a graj, which looks like a cheese grater; and other percussion instruments. To their left, four more guys stand shoulder to shoulder and play the crying melodies I love on the konet, a long metal trumpet with a bell at its end.

"What does 'Gran Bwa' mean?" Alex asks.

"It come from the French, '*Grand Bois*,'" I say.

"Great woods?"

"I forgot, you know French," I say. Alex smiles, looking a little proud. "It's more like 'great tree,' though. Or 'big tree.'" Still a trace of a smile on his lips. It is a nice smile. He is a handsome boy, I can't help notice. "So, this place is named after the Haitian spirit Gran Bwa. He's very important in vodou, and the band pick him as their patron spirit. Gran Bwa look like a giant tree. You see that rock over there, with the face carved into it?"

Alex arches his neck to get a view of the Gran Bwa sculpture to the right of the band. "Yeah, I see it. That's him?"

"Yes. You can see how powerful he is, how fierce. Gran Bwa has control over all the wilderness. So he is a bit wild and unpredictable. Filled with energy and magic, too. Like the music, no?"

I nod to Jou Jou, who works his mouth along with the thick rhythm, like chewing beef jerky. His dreadlocks, not quite shoulder-length yet, dance along in time. Maybe this is what Gran Bwa would have looked like when he was here on Earth, filled with life and unpredictable energy. The sky is almost completely dark now. The snare drummer bobs his shoulders, and the sax player leans back, exposing his throat. The man playing the salt shaker dances toward the middle of the circle, wearing the grin of an elf, full of mischief. "Whoa-ah! Come on, come on!" he shouts, pushing the musicians to play louder, tighter.

"That's Fabian, the one with the knit cap," I lean over and tell Alex. "He started Rara Gran Bwa, long time ago. He's the leader."

"Yeah, I can tell," he whispers. "He's amazing. He's just playing that little salt shaker, but he's incredible. It's like he's conducting."

"That's right," I say, smiling. "Exactly."

For a moment, Jou Jou looks at Alex and me again, or maybe at a spot of the tree directly behind us. He bobs his head left and right, sometime closing his eyes, so deeply under the music's spell, the crazy fool doesn't seem to recognize his own sister.

"How long has he been playing the drums?" Alex asks me.

"About three years now, I think. I'm not sure, exactly. He came to America four years before me."

"That's all, a few years? He's so good!"

"Rara music, if you're Haitian, it's in your blood. Jou

Jou, he pick up the rhythms faster than most. An outsider would never learn so quick, but he's been hearing the music his whole life."

"He's fantastic. They all are. I've never heard anything like it. Do they teach it in the schools there?"

"Rara? In the schools? They would never allow it. Rara is street music. My grandfather, my mother, my uncle . . . they *hate* this music. They think Jou Jou throw away his life by doing this."

"Really? What's wrong with it? It's just . . . music."

"Yes, but to them it's *musique démoniaque.* Devil's music, you see?"

"Not really."

"The Christians in Haiti, they think the people who make this music in Haiti for centuries are the low people, the poor. They think this music, it is *vodou* music that the uneducated and ignorant use to call bad spirits."

"And Haitians here in Brooklyn think that, too?"

"Some of them, yes. Mostly the older ones, like my uncle." Oh, I shouldn't have said that. Too private. It is not good to talk badly about an elder.

"That's too bad."

He shakes his head. Maybe he doesn't believe that anyone could hold such harsh opinions about something as innocent as music. It's only sound floating on the air, after all. But this is another thing about Americans I have noticed:

they want to think everyone around them is so happy, living in harmony. They choose not to see the walls that separate people from each other, these walls that exist everywhere one cares to look.

In another minute, the song continues with four long blasts from the konets. Fabian, dancing and calling out from the center of the circle, tosses his head into the air to cue that the end is near and finally kicks powerfully with his right leg. The entire band syncs when he brings his foot to the ground, and the piece is complete. The spectators, including Alex and me, erupt in cheers.

"Do they ever play concerts?" Alex asks. "You know, in clubs or wherever?"

Suddenly, I remember what it felt like the first time Alex spoke to me, before those cruel boys teased him about the cards. I had forgotten how nice the conversation was, before others had to spoil it.

"In the past, they play lots of house parties. Like, in the community, here in Flatbush. And benefit concerts for kids, things like this to buy presents for them at Christmas, you know. But now, since the earthquake, they getting much more popular. Clubs in Brooklyn and Manhattan, good clubs. They might even be invited to the New Orleans Jazz Festival this year. We will see."

Jou Jou approaches us, his expression soft and relaxed again, as it was during our walk.

"What you think, sister?" he asks, kissing me on both cheeks.

"*Très bien*, Jou Jou. Beautiful. Rara Gran Bwa sound fantastic, as always."

"And you, Alex? You like the music?"

"Yeah, it was incredible," Alex says. "You guys are amazing. My sister plays the cello. But it's nothing like this!"

Jou Jou rears his head back to laugh. "Now that's some positive feedback, man. Thank you. I like this boy, Bijou. He's good."

I grit my teeth and let the comment pass. Now I *know* he's trying to torture me.

"Do you guys rehearse a lot?" Alex asks.

"Well, this isn't a practice. This just a little jam session at the Gran Bwa here. But yeah, we practice, too, over on Church Avenue. You should come sometime."

"I'd like to."

"Jou Jou, we not done yet, man," says Darly, the petwo player. He wears a sour look on his face, as always. "Get back here."

"Yes, man, I'm comin'," Jou Jou says. He gives us a look of pretend-scared, rolls his eyes, and heads back toward the band.

"Okay, get in here, brothers," Fabian says, kneeling and extending his hand. The band members surround him like football players in a huddle. "One band, one sound!"

The band repeats, "One band, one sound!"
Fabian yells, "Rara, Rara, Rara Gran Bwa!"
And the band repeats, "Rara, Rara, Rara Gran Bwa!"

...———ℓℓℓℓℓ———...

Alex's phone buzzes: a text. "Oops, that's my mom," he says. "I've gotta get going."

"Time for dinner?" I ask.

"Yep. I didn't realize how late it had gotten."

I look at my watch: 8:15. "Oh no, me too!" If I don't get home in fifteen minutes, my uncle will go crazy. And it's more than a mile's walk to get home. Forgetting about Alex for the moment, I wave to get Jou Jou's attention. "Jou Jou! We need to get out of here, and right now!"

"Okay, okay!" Jou Jou calls back, laughing as usual, not one concern in the world. *"J'arrive, j'arrive!" I'm coming.*

Finally, after a few high fives with his bandmates, my brother is by my side. We say a quick good-bye to Alex, and we are running, running, racing to get home before my uncle's deadline.

12

Making the Call

Nomura, Ira, and I eat our lunches on the roof playground, looking down on the shops of Montague Street while a bunch of sixth graders play handball behind us. Last year, the three of us were obsessed with handball, lining up along with every other guy in our class for a chance to take on the champion (usually Trevor or Greg Vargas, and every once in a while, Nomura, who sports a wicked backhand). Now, the sixth graders look silly for being so into it. Why do they care so much about such a stupid game?

We peer through the bars of the rooftop fence, and I tell Ira and Nomura everything that happened at the park.

"She really kissed you?" Ira asks, eyes bugging.

"Yeah," I say. "I mean, it happened pretty quickly. But . . . yeah." Was it a "real" kiss, though? When you've never been kissed before, it's hard to know.

"You don't sound so sure," Nomura says. "Was it on the

lips, or was it like the type of kiss your grandmother would give you?"

"Gross!" Ira says, and we all laugh.

"No lips, just a kiss on the cheek," I say. "But she did it twice."

"For real?" Ira says. "Twice?"

"Yeah." I remember the way she turned each cheek toward me, like she was offering me a small gift. And I remember the smell of her, like flowers, and almonds, and shampoo.

"Why would she kiss you twice, though?" Ira asks.

I shrug. Once, twice, who cares? But I hope there are more kisses in my near future. I hope not for two, but for two hundred, two thousand, and beyond.

"I wouldn't get too excited about it," Nomura says. "It's probably what everybody does in Haiti. You know, to say hello and good-bye."

"Could be." I hadn't thought about that before; it could only be a custom. Does that mean it was no big deal for her to kiss me? It definitely felt like a big deal to *me*.

"That's how the French do it," Nomura says.

"*'Do it,'*" Ira repeats, making it sound dirty and weird.

"Shut up," I say, punching him in the arm. "Don't talk about it like that."

"God," he says, rubbing the sore spot. "You didn't have to hit me."

"Sorry," I say. "But can you please try to be cool about this?"

Ira doesn't say a thing, and I can tell he has no idea what I mean. Asking him to be cool is like asking him to speak fluent Mandarin; it's a skill he simply doesn't have.

I turn to Nomura. "The French kiss on both sides of the cheek, *every* time they say hello and good-bye? That sounds like an awful lot of work."

He shrugs. "It's just the way things are over there."

"Doesn't 'French kiss' mean you use your tongue?" asks Ira. We ignore him.

"During the kiss," I remember, picturing it in my head, "she kind of rested her hand on my shoulder."

"Huh? How do you mean?" Nomura asks.

"You want me to show you?"

"Umm, no, not really!" Nomura laughs. Then he pushes his glasses up higher on his nose and says, "Do you mean she kind of leaned on you for balance?"

"Yeah, I guess." I hate how he breaks everything down until it sounds so practical and rational. In his way of looking at things, the kiss didn't mean anything. But it did mean something to *me*, and now I feel like my best friend is taking it away from me.

"Listen, Mr. Logical," I say. "I was there. You weren't. There was a . . . feeling. She felt so . . . close to me."

"You should have grabbed her and French-kissed her

right there!" Ira yells. Before I can even think of punching his arm, he holds up his hands defensively. "Sorry, sorry!" he says.

I shake my head. When's he going to grow up?

"So, when are you going to ask her out?" Nomura asks.

"What? You mean, on a date?" I say.

"Of course, on a date. What else?"

"I don't know, I don't think—"

"Trust me, this is the move now." Nomura is in full-on expert mode. Where does he get this stuff? "This is what you have to do."

"Like you've ever gone on a date. Or even asked for one. You're giving me the same advice that you've seen best friends give in every bad romance movie you've ever seen."

"I don't watch *romance* movies."

"You totally do! You cried at the end of *The Notebook*. Which sucked, by the way."

"I've never even seen that movie."

"Right. I'll bet you could recite it line for line."

"Anyway, none of this changes the fact that my advice is a hundred percent sound," Nomura says. Now he's cramming his face with Fig Newtons. It annoys me how casual he is, as if we're talking about a homework assignment. It's my *life* we're discussing here.

"And now's the time to act. I mean, just call her."

"But I don't have her number."

Nomura sighs like a bored teacher, tired of explaining the same concept for the thousandth time. "Of course you do."

"Uh, no. I'm pretty sure I don't."

"Alex," Nomura says, "aren't Ira and I your best friends?"

Ira looks over at me, wondering if it's still true. "Yes," I say, and he smiles, happy to be reassured. "Of course."

"And as your best friends, don't you think we're going to do everything in our power to help you out?"

"Well, yeah, I guess. But . . . how?"

"We got her number." Nomura looks superproud.

"Really? How?"

Nomura laughs and reads it to me. "I've got my sources," he says, by which he means Mary Agnes, I'm guessing. "Now it's your move."

"Go for it," says Ira.

.... ℓℓℓℓℓ ....

At home, all I can do for an entire twenty-five minutes is stare at the phone. Am I really going to call? It's a bold move, and one that could easily backfire.

I look at my phone as if seeing it for the first time. The cleanly polished surface, with my own reflection staring back at me. The shiny power button.

Twenty-five minutes can sure go slowly when you're trying to make a decision.

.....—&&&&&—.....

I go to the kitchen and make myself a chicken sandwich. I spread the mustard as slowly as I can, trying to buy time, trying to think. I put on lettuce and some sharp cheddar. I cut the wheat bread into halves with a knife with teeth on it.

I pour myself a Pepsi from the bottle and drink it.

Then, I think, *Why not a cup of tea?* Even though I never drink tea. But drinking tea is good for thinking and making decisions, so I let it brew, nice and slow.

.....—&&&&&—.....

I think about calling Nomura but decide not to.

.....—&&&&&—.....

I check the time. It's 3:59. Dolly could be home any minute, and as soon as she is, it's going to be tough to find the privacy to call. If I go to my room, I'll have to close the door, and if I close the door, she'll ask me what I was doing in secret. And if she starts grilling me for answers, she'll wind up guessing what I'm up to. It happens every time.

Ack, I should just call! Bijou's just a person, like me.

.....—&&&&&—.....

It's 4:11. I should call, already.

Calling is something the old Alex Schrader would never dream of doing. But maybe it's time for a new Alex, I think, a more courageous Alex who doesn't let his mom buy his jeans for him. Who talks to a girl off the top of his head instead of looking at notes on index cards. Who actually, in Ira's words, *goes for it*.

·····ₑₑₑₑ·····

At 4:17, I punch in the number:

718-555-6566

I stare at it for a full sixty seconds, knowing that as soon as I press the button, my life could drastically change again within moments. I feel like the president of the United States, with my hand hovering over The Button, wondering whether I'm really ready to set this chain of events in motion.

·····ₑₑₑₑ·····

I press call.

 13

Haitian, Haitian, Go Back to Your Nation

It's lunchtime. Mary Agnes, Maricel, and I are walking down Montague Street with our sandwiches. Just strolling, enjoying a bit of nice weather, at last. It's almost the end of March, and this is the first day since I moved here that I remember the sun tickling my skin. Ah, I hope this means spring is here.

"Did you know they have a playground up there?" Maricel asks, nodding upward.

"Who?" I have no idea who she is talking about.

"The boys, silly," Mary Agnes says. "St. Chris's."

Maricel points, and I follow her finger to the rooftop of the school, where I see a fence that extends up past the top of the building by at least the height of a full-grown man.

"Alex and John and Ira are probably looking down at us right now," Mary Agnes says.

"That is a bit . . . how do you say? Creepy?" I say.

"It's not creepy," Mary Agnes says. "It's cute." But to Mary Agnes, everything is cute, no?

"Why can't they be friends with someone else?" asks Maricel. "Someone attractive? Who's not my brother?"

"Feeling left out?" Mary Agnes teases.

"Alex likes Bijou, and you like Nomura," Maricel says. "Who have I got to like? Nobody."

I repeat the phrase in my head: *Alex likes Bijou.* I like this. I like this *being liked.* What I don't like, though, is not knowing what it means, where it will lead. I can never be with this boy, can I? It seems so impossible.

"Someone'll come along for you, Mari," Mary Agnes says. "But let's get back to Bijou." She turns to me and raises an eyebrow. "Alex does like Bijou. But does Bijou like Alex?"

I can't believe she is asking me. "This is silly," I say. "Of course not."

"Look at her," says Maricel. "Is she blushing?"

"She totally is," says Mary Agnes. "Because she totally likes Alex Schrader."

I have finished my sandwich. I roll the plastic wrap into a ball and put it back in the paper sack. "All right," I say. "Maybe a little."

They both laugh.

"Very nice," Mary Agnes says. "Everything is going according to plan."

"How do you mean, 'according to plan'?" I ask.

We walk by a brownstone stoop, only a block away from

St. Catherine's now, which is good, because we have only three minutes before lunch is over. What is less good: Angela Gudrun and Jenna Minaya are sitting on this stoop. As we walk by, they stare at us, and we stare at them. Then, as we pass them, they follow directly behind us.

"What plan is that, Mary Agnes?" Angela asks.

Mary Agnes says nothing. It's the best thing to do when these two are around: just ignore them, and they will walk away soon enough.

"I'll bet it has to do with Alex," Angela says. "You know, Mr. Index Cards."

"Right, him," Jenna says. "He's kind of cute, but he acts like he's still in sixth grade."

"Try fifth," Angela says. "Zero confidence."

I can feel Mary Agnes, to my right, about to say something. Her whole body is as tense as stretched wire. I touch the back of her elbow, a signal: *Don't do anything.*

Then, from nowhere, Jenna says, or actually, *sings*: "Haitian, Haitian, go back to your nation."

At first, I do not even understand her words. But I follow my own advice. I don't say or do anything.

Jenna laughs at my silence and repeats the rhyme again, like a chant: "Haitian, Haitian, go back to your nation."

She says it three times, and Angela joins her the last time, laughing so hard she can barely say the words.

Finally, I cannot stop myself. Only a few meters from

the school steps, I stop, turn around, and look directly at her. "Stupid girl," I say, pointing my finger at her, "do you even have any idea of the words you are saying?"

"What did you call me?" Jenna asks, taking a step closer.

Before I can respond, an entire fifth-grade class comes running down the steps, some of them slipping between Jenna and me. I look up to see Miss Williams, who is peering down at us, trying to see what's going on.

"Everything okay down there, Ms. Minaya?" the teacher asks.

"Yep!" Jenna says brightly. Then she whispers under her breath, "We'll settle this later," and runs up the steps, two at a time.

Sometimes I do not understand people. I do not understand them at all. Why would she tell me to go back to *my* country? Isn't America supposed to be the place where everyone comes from somewhere else?

Once we are inside, Jenna and Angela walk in the opposite direction.

"Bijou," says Mary Agnes, "I'm so sorry."

"Sorry for what?" I ask. "You didn't do anything."

The first time we visited America, Maman told me there might be people in America who would not like me because I am black or because I am Haitian. She told me that for most Americans the word "Haiti" means only three things: vodou, the way it is seen only in movies, with snakes, little dolls, and evil curses; poor people, like the ones who lived in poverty well before the earthquake; and that murdering disease AIDS. She said that some people think like this because they are ignorant, and it makes them feel better about themselves to look at me in this way. To insult me to my face so that they might feel better about their own sorry selves. But this is the first time that I see it is actually happening.

It is one thing to think about the possibility of something happening, and another, quite different thing to actually have it happen. Oh, how I wish Maman were here. Or Jou Jou. Or even Tonton Pierre.

…——ₑₑₑₑ——…

"How was school, my love?" Marie Claire asks when I get home.

"Very good, *tante*," I say, lying. "I'm going to go and do some homework now."

She smiles at me so peacefully that I almost believe my own story, and soon enough, I am doing my prealgebra problems, *almost* able to give the boring work my full concentration.

In ten minutes, the phone rings. My uncle, he has a cell phone, but still he keeps also the old phone. He says you never know when there might be an emergency and we need this phone.

I never answer it, though—only once, last week, Mary
Agnes called me to say hello, but other than that, I never
get calls—so I stay in my room. It rings and rings and
rings.

After the fifth ring, I hear Marie Claire pick it up. I go
back to my homework.

In another moment, though, Marie Claire knocks on
my door.

"Bijou?" she calls. I run to the door and open it. Marie
Claire puts her hand over the phone and whispers, *"C'est
un garçon."* *It's a boy.*

She looks at me as if I have brought a boy in the house
and am hiding him under the covers. I say nothing but plead
with my eyes: *Don't tell Tonton. I did not ask this boy to
call. It is not my fault.*

Marie Claire shakes her head, looking truly sad. She
hands me the phone but goes nowhere. Isn't she going
to give me any privacy? She's not just going to stand there,
is she?

Marie Claire does not move.

"Hallo? Who is this, please?" I look up at my aunt. She
raises her eyebrows: *Get on with it, child.*

"It's Alex," he says.

I say nothing.

"You know, from yesterday? In the park?" he asks.

"I know, I know, of course," I say. I try to sound stern

and upset, the way Pierre would expect me to. "But how
did you get this number? And why are you calling me here?"

"*C'est pour école,*" I say to Marie Claire. "*Oui, c'est un
garçon, mais c'est pour lycee.*" *Yes, it's a boy, but it's for
school.*

Oh, why did he have to call? Doesn't he understand how
much trouble I could get in for this?

"Alex, thank you for giving me the assignment," I say,
hoping that Marie Claire will believe this silly lie, or at
least ignore it.

"What assignment?" he asks. I hope she didn't hear that.
I just keep talking.

I continue, "But you cannot call me at home. Ever."

"Oh no. I'm really sorry."

"It is all right. But you understand now, all right?"

"Sure, sure," he says. "Hey, I hope . . . I'm really—"

But I hang up before he finishes. I have no choice. I will
have to explain later—and hope that he understands.

14

Project Bijou

It's been a week since the phone call, and I'm thinking of Bijou a little less each day.

That's a total lie; it's the exact opposite. It's actually getting worse.

Every day, all day, I go over each detail of the dance, of the nightmarish call, and think: *What could I have done differently? And how could I have shown myself to her in a way that would make her like me?*

I told Nomura that I'd had a "feeling" talking to Bijou at the dance, before everything went wrong, and at the park. And I did. I can't put it into words, but even though I seem to be jinxed every time I try to move this thing forward, I still can't help but have the *feeling* that Bijou came into my life for a reason. A *feeling* that we are going to be part of each other's lives in some little way.

Does that make me crazy? Or a stalker? Please, God, tell

me this is a *feeling* I can trust. Because if this doesn't work out, I'm going to put my *feelings* away for a nice, long time.

Adios, feelings. Or better yet: *Au revoir, sentiments.*

This morning, I grab my gym bag from my locker just before PE, and a small envelope falls to the floor. Someone has folded it in half and pushed it through the vent. My last name is written on the front, carefully constructed in large block letters and viciously underlined three times. I rip open the envelope and unfold the note, which has been printed ultraneatly on unlined paper.

Don't waste your time on that stupid girl.
She's a liar.

That's it, just those two sentences! Like a character in a movie, I look one way, then the other, like the person who wrote this could actually be stupid enough to wait and watch me open it. Everyone up and down the hall is going about their regular business, of course, not paying attention to the fact that my jaw is scraping the floor. *That stupid girl?* Who do I know who would write this? Rocky? Trevor? Maybe, but *why*? Why not say it to my face?

I fold the note and tuck it into my pocket, then close my locker and go to PE.

_____ ℓℓℓℓℓ _____

"What's wrong?" Nomura asks, chewing what looks like one of those date bars they sell at every Brooklyn bodega. We're eating our lunches on a bench on the corner of Henry and Clark, looking at all the college kids flowing in and out of an NYU dorm building. Half of them are holding hands, gushy-gushy in love and practically skipping down the sidewalk. It feels like they're purposely mocking me, rubbing my failure with Bijou in my face.

"You okay?" Nomura asks. I don't tell him I'm sad about Bijou, and I don't tell him about the note. If I don't tell anybody about it, then the only two people this is real for are the guy who wrote it and me. And for now, that's exactly how I want to keep it.

Anyway, Nomura's busy telling me about his Theory of Fate.

"You're a fatalist," he says.

"A *what*-alist?" I say. "Chew your food, and *then* talk, man. I can't hear a thing you're saying."

"Things don't work out so great for most people who believe in fate."

"Bijou and I would work out great, if only she'd give me a chance. I can feel it."

"Look at Tchaikovsky. Or Baudelaire. You don't want to go down that road, believe me."

"I don't want fate; I want a date. And so far, by the way, all the wisdom you've got about how to deal with girls has been completely wrong. The index cards, the phone call . . ."

"I'm just the facilitator." Nomura's phone rings. He checks a text and puts it back in his pocket.

"Speak English, please."

"All I've done is make suggestions and given you a friendly push here and there."

"Well, it's not working."

"Fair enough." He takes one last gulp of mango-coconut water, tipping his head back and tapping the bottom of the bottle to make sure he doesn't miss a drop. "I do have one more trick up my sleeve, though."

"Oh yeah?" I can't help but smile. Even in the lowest of times, Nomura entertains me. He just does. "When am I going to see this trick?"

"In about fifteen seconds."

"What?"

"It . . . well, *she*, is walking right at us."

It's Mary Agnes, her eyes sparkling with ambition as she approaches our bench.

"Hi, guys," she says.

"Hi," we both answer.

"Well, Alex, are you going to move over so I can sit, or are you going to keep staring at me like I've been beamed down from Mars?"

"Sorry," I say, moving to the right so that she can sandwich herself between us.

"Okay, here's the deal," she says. "Bijou likes you."

"Really?" I get so excited, I almost stand up. Nomura gives me a look, like, *That was embarrassing, you're so busted.*

"Well, she might not know it yet, but I do."

Oh, great. Another know-it-all. Another Nomura. "What exactly does *that* mean?" I ask. "What did she say, exactly?"

"She didn't say anything, but she didn't have to; I can tell." She thinks for a second. "But she can't go around blabbing about it, because in her culture, dating is totally not allowed. And I mean, like, *forbidden.*"

"Yeah, I've gotten that. I actually tried to call her. It . . . didn't go well."

"Like the forbidden fruit," Nomura says, savoring the words. "Like the apple that Adam and Eve couldn't resist taking a big, fat bite out of."

"Huh?" Mary Agnes asks. Neither one of us has any idea what Nomura's talking about. "More like something that is so off-limits that she needs to figure out for herself whether it's worth the risk. And by the way, calling her at home? That wasn't a great move." I flash Nomura a look of my own: *Thanks a lot.*

"So how, exactly, do they keep boys and girls from hanging out?" I ask. "I mean, look at us. We're on a public street, just talking. No illegal activity taking place here, right? Nothing scandalous?"

"Bijou says the only times she can even talk to a boy

she's not related to is at church, at school—as in, within the actual, physical walls of the school building, which is pretty much impossible given that there are no boys allowed in St. Cat's—or at a school-sponsored event."

"And it's not like I can just walk into a Haitian church in Flatbush," I say, "and tell everybody that God spoke to me in a vision and told me to join up."

"True," Mary Agnes says, laughing.

"Well, there's not another dance until May," Nomura says. "But Musicale's on April twentieth. Maybe you guys should do something for it."

Spring Musicale is the one nondance opportunity each year for us to do stuff with the St. Cat's girls. Cross-school collaborations are allowed, even encouraged, so each year dozens of kids sign up. St. Cat's lets us use the rehearsal rooms in its basement, and supervision is relatively hands-off, so each Musicale team usually signs up for hours and hours of so-called rehearsal. Really, though, it's a chance for the boys and girls who like each other to hang out.

I hadn't even thought of Musicale as a possibility. Perhaps because I can't act and have no musical talent. Or any talent, for that matter.

"That's your grand plan?" I say. "Bijou and me, doing something for Musicale? What would we do?"

"Maybe we could *all* do something together," Mary Agnes says. "You and Bijou, me and John."

For a second, I don't know who she means by "John."

But then I see her looking at Nomura. She's biting her lip, waiting for him to respond. Could Nomura actually make Mary Agnes nervous? Could Nomura make *anyone* nervous?

"Maybe," Nomura says, rushing. "But no, Alex, that's not the grand plan. The grand plan is a date. A date with you and Bijou."

"Didn't we figure out that there is no way whatsoever for that to happen?" I ask.

"We did," says Mary Agnes.

"But now you're saying there *is* going to be a date after all?"

"Yep." Mary Agnes positively glows with this news.

"We found a work-around," says Nomura.

"Yeah?" I say. "I'm waiting."

"A chaperoned date," says Mary Agnes.

"What's that?" I ask. "Like a group date? Like you guys come, and Maricel and Ira?"

"No, man," Nomura says. "You're not getting it. It's not just boys she can't see. Maricel and Mary Agnes are as off-limits as you and me."

"So, what, then? Who's going to supervise?"

"Her brother," Mary Agnes says.

"Jou Jou?" I ask. "Jou Jou's going to hang out with us . . . on a date? No way will Bijou ever go for that."

"It's taken care of," Mary Agnes says. "I know, it sounds a little weird—"

"A lot weird," says Nomura. "But it's the only way this can happen."

"It gives her an excuse, right?" says Mary Agnes. "She's not going to tell her aunt and uncle exactly what she'll be doing. But later, if her uncle asks her where she was, or what she was doing, she could say she was hanging out with him—"

"And she wouldn't be lying," I say.

"Exactly," Mary Agnes says.

Fine, then. I'm going to have to trust this redhead and hope for the best.

"At least it's her brother, not her uncle, right?"

"Okay, I get it, I guess," I say. "And she's cool with this? She's into it?"

"Yeah."

"And that means she likes me, you think?"

"Or she might be slowly falling for you, and those little puppy-dog faces you make anytime she's around," Nomura says.

"We really can't say for sure," Mary Agnes says, laughing.

"We?" I ask. "You guys been having fun collaborating on this little project?"

"Project Bijou," Nomura says, in his dorky "creepy" voice. Mary Agnes is falling . . . for *this*?

"Hey, you should be grateful," Mary Agnes says. "I wish I had this kind of help with my own love life."

Is she saying she *wants* help? I give Nomura a sidelong glance, but he either ignores it or pretends to.

"Just meet her on the—"

"Meet *them*," Nomura says. "There'll be two of them."

"—meet *them* at the Parkside Q stop tomorrow, at three thirty."

"Okay, Parkside it is," I say, noticing that this will put us smack in the middle of the part of Flatbush that my mom has flat-out forbidden me to visit. "And Mary Agnes . . . thanks!"

"Good luck," she says, smiling. "You're going to need it."

"Boy, is he ever," says Nomura.

"Thanks for the vote of confidence," I say, punching him in the bicep.

15

Dollar Van

This is not how I imagined my first date with a boy.

First, I didn't picture a boy at all; I imagined a man, or someone at least eighteen. And I imagined myself as a full-grown woman, too, tall and filled with confidence. I would be wearing a beautiful, elegant outfit while my date escorted me to a fancy restaurant with a view of the water. Instead, I'm wearing a big winter coat, black with fat, puffy sleeves. And I'm waiting for a strange American boy to emerge from a grimy subway station in this new, freezing city I'm trying to call home. *Trying.*

Ah, there is Alex, walking out of the station. He wears blue jeans, like everyone does here, and a light-green jacket. He must have changed into these clothes specially for me. I wish I had thought of that. Next to him I will look so silly in my St. Catherine's uniform.

I know I should go greet him, but I'll wait here a little bit longer. It can be fun to spot someone before they know you are near; it's the best way to see what they are really like. Alex puts his hands in his pockets, then takes them out, looking around for me but trying not to be noticed.

He walks toward an advertisement, a poster under glass, and stares at it. What does he see there? But now he pulls up his hands and smooths out his hair. He is not looking at the poster; he is making sure his hair is straight, that he has nothing in his teeth. He wants to make sure he looks good for me!

"Hello, Alex," I say, at last walking up to him.

"Hi!" Alex says, a little too loudly. "How are you?"

"I am . . . good," I say. "I wish I had brought some other clothes, though."

"No, you look good," Alex says. "You . . . always look good."

Oh my Lord, did he really just say that? I have to look away for a moment.

His eyes are very pretty, I have to admit. The sun touches them, and white light dances off the blue (or is it green?) near their center. For the first time, I notice how tall he is. Most boys are shorter than me; not this one.

"Is . . . everything all set up?" Alex looks around, to the side and above my shoulder, wondering why I am alone, since that was not the agreement.

"Yes. You see, across the street?"

Alex waves across the street. "So, that's Jou Jou's van? He uses it for music, for the band?"

"No, he drives the dollar van."

"What's a dollar van?"

"You've never taken one? But you live very close to Flat-bush Avenue, *non*?"

How can Alex live right next to Flatbush Avenue, how could he have seen the dollar vans a thousand times in his life, and never realized what they were for? It is as if we live in two different countries: not America and Haiti, but white Flatbush and black Flatbush. They are just as differ-ent, and just as far apart.

"Well, pretty close, yeah. People ride these . . . dollar vans . . . on Flatbush?"

"Dollar van is the *only* thing people ride on Flatbush." As we cross the street, I smile to let him know it is okay he doesn't know. After all, think of all the things *I* do not know about Brooklyn. "They go to places the city's buses don't, and you can pay a dollar, fifty cents, or even less. And the people are nice. Usually."

"Hello, Alex!" Jou Jou says, jumping out of the van to let us in.

"Hey, Jou Jou," Alex says, smiling. "How's it going?"

"Good, man, good. Glad to see you."

Alex looks more relaxed already. My brother has this

talent, this gift to help people feel at ease, that I have never had. Everyone loves Jou Jou, right away.

"Okay now," Jou Jou says as he gets back into the driver's seat and puts on his seat belt. There are three rows of seats; Alex and I are all the way in the back. "You two enjoy yourselves as my special guests while Jou Jou make himself a little money."

My brother drives down Church toward Flatbush Avenue, where two older Haitian ladies and a young mother and her little boy are waiting. The boy has a black parka with large yellow stripes across its front. He wears no gloves and shivers with cold. Three years old, four maybe, he struggles with his jacket, cannot get it off without help.

"Whachoo doin', little one?" the mother teases her son, laughing at his long jacket sleeves. "You the abominable snowman." It is still strange to me, so odd, to see West Indian people in this cold northern weather. We are too warm-blooded for this stinging wind.

"Praise the Lord, he tryin' to stay warm," one of the old ladies says, giggling, as they sit down in the middle row, the one in front of us. "Hallo, Joseph, how are you?"

"Good, Mrs. Jenkins. You get comfortable and rest your feet, now."

Behind us, still on the street, a man in a wheelchair screams into a pay phone while finishing off a hamburger. He wears a camouflage Windbreaker with the hood up and squeezes his legs together at the knees, like a child who has to use the toilet. The hamburger gone, he lets the McDonald's wrapper fall off his fingers, and the yellow paper flies away on the wind.

"You take this van all the time?" Alex asks.

"Every day after school," I say. "Jou Jou, he pick me up from Parkside and take me home."

The old ladies ask us where we go to school and are very happy when we tell them St. Christopher's and St. Catherine's. But Jou Jou has just picked up an old black man, an American, not a West Indian, and the man loudly interrupts the conversation.

"In my time," he says, "they don't let no black girl go to no St. Catherine school."

"Progress, sir, progress," says one of the old ladies. They all know one another; I don't know their names, but I've seen them in Jou Jou's van many times before.

"Some things change; some things, they stay the same," he says. "Bet they don't treat her like they treat the white girls."

"They treat her fine; they good *Christian* people," says the old lady, turning around and grinning at me. I can't help but notice they would rather argue about how I am treated at school than ask me myself.

"You ever take the dollar van before, boy?" the old man asks Alex.

"First time," he answers.

"How you travel regular, young man? Town car?" The man has a gleam in his eye. He's only having fun, but Alex doesn't understand.

"Uhh, no. Subway. Or bus, sometimes."

Jou Jou yells from the driver's seat, "We better than the bus! More cheaper, and faster!"

The old ladies get off at Rogers Avenue, followed by the man, as well as the mother and son. "Good-bye, children!" one of the ladies says to us. "We take ol' Grumpy with us, so you can enjoy yourselves now." Both women laugh, throwing their heads into the air.

All the passengers are gone now, and Jou Jou ignores a couple of people who try to flag him down. "We on our own now," he says. "Let's show Alex something fun."

We are at the corner of Church and Nostrand, driving east. There's a huge sign on the second floor of a brick building that reads IMMIGRATION in hand-painted letters, advertising for a business that doesn't seem to exist, since all that's left below is the Golden Krust bakery. The shop awnings, flags with bright, clashing colors, scream out, fighting for attention: MARIB'S UNIVERSAL MIX, OLIVE'S APPAREL CENTER (LINGERIE! UNIFORMS!), EMMANUEL GOSPEL BOOK STORE (CHRIST IS KING!), and every third business is a roti shop. I see Alex looking out the window, taking in all the details, his eyes hungry.

"You want a roti?" I ask.

"A what?" Alex asks.

"You live in Flatbush your whole life and you never had a buss-up-shut roti?" Jou Jou says from the front.

"Say it one more time," Alex says.

"A *buss-up-shut roti*," I say.

"I don't even know how to pronounce that, never mind eat it. Is it Haitian?"

"No, from Trinidad most times, or Jamaica. But it's still good. Jou Jou introduce it to me."

"Okay, that's it, I'm turning around," Jou Jou says, heading back toward Flatbush Avenue. "We goin' to Trini-Daddy's, right now, before somebody else flags me down."

He pulls into the first parking place he sees, claps his hands together, and says, "You want what for filling? Chicken? Shrimp? Goat?"

"For real, goat?" Alex asks.

"Watch, he's going to have chicken," I say, shaking my head in pretend disapproval.

"You Americans. So predictable," Jou Jou says, turning to face us from the front seat.

"I'll take the goat," Alex says. He pushes his chin out, like: *Ha, take that!*

"Really?" Jou Jou asks, laughing. "You want to try it?"

"Yep, goat it is." Then he raises his eyebrows. "Chicken's boring, anyway."

"Okay, three goat buss-up-shuts, comin' up," Jou Jou says, shutting the door. "You two stay in the van. I be right back." I can't help looking around us, outside the van. What if someone saw Alex and me alone here, together? It's only for a moment, but no one would know that. The news would travel back to my uncle like this: "BIJOU WAS ALONE WITH A BOY IN THE BACK OF A CAR!" And you can imagine what Tonton Pierre would do.

My brother jogs across the street, bouncing with each step. He sidesteps the lovely tall tree that stands in front of Trini-Daddy's. "Jou Jou likes you," I say. I don't say that *I* like him, please notice, although I must admit, I do; but I can't make things *too* easy for him yet, can I?

"He's so cool," Alex says. "You're lucky to have a brother like him."

"You think you would rather go out with Jou Jou, then?" I ask. I can't resist; it's too easy.

"What? No!" He colors past red now, into purple, more eggplant than tomato.

"Don't be embarrassed. I'm just teasing." I try to reassure him with a smile. I spend a lot of time reassuring Alex, it seems. "You color so easy, Alex."

"I know, I do it all the time," he says. "But doesn't everybody, at least sometimes?"

"Black people, we do not color. And if we do, it hides itself better. For this, it's good to have dark skin."

"Yeah, I guess so."

Alex smiles and looks out the window, and I notice how long his eyelashes are. Alex, he looks still so like a boy, with ears a bit too large for his head, and that distracted look on his face, like he's always thinking of something other than what is right in front of him. But those eyes. He could melt any girl with those eyes.

"So you live with your aunt and uncle, is that right?" Alex asks.

"Yes," I reply. Oh no, here we go. "Marie Claire and Pierre. He is the older brother of my maman."

He is getting nervous again, I can tell. He doesn't know what is all right to ask. "So you still have family, back home?"

"My mother, my grandfather, they're from Port-au-Prince." Why is he asking so many questions? Americans are too curious, if you ask me. "What about you, Alex?" I try to keep myself calm and make *him* talk about *his* life. Anything to get the attention off me and my family!

"Well, I live with my mom and my sister, Dahlia. We call her Dolly."

"And your father?" Now it is my turn to be so curious, so nosy.

"He . . . left. A long time ago. I barely even remember him."

"Really?" I say. I can't help but be surprised. "Me too. I cannot even remember what Papa looks like sometimes."

"I'm sorry."

I laugh. "I'm sorry, too. What is the expression? We are in the same boat?"

"I've spent even less time in boats than I have in dollar vans." Alex laughs.

And now we stay silent for a moment. Outside, two men speak loudly in Spanish. I can't tell whether it is an argument or friendly joking. Everyone in Flatbush always is yelling, whether they are happy or they are angry or they are sad.

"One more thing," Alex says. He has that look again. What is he going to say now? "I just want to make sure, you know, you're okay with this? This chaperoned thing?"

"How do you mean?"

"I don't know, but I hope I'm not making you do something you don't want to do, like an obligation. And for Jou Jou, too. I mean, the way he has to come along. I don't exactly go on lots of dates, but this is kind of weird, right?"

"Not at all. I wanted to see you and . . . get to know you better." All right, this is partly a lie. It took Mary Agnes three days to persuade me to do this. But it's not a lie if I'm honestly saying what I feel right now, is it?

"Really?"

"Yes, really. And this must be strange for you, to have my brother with us. But you must understand, for Haitians, we absolutely cannot see other people outside the family. Especially girls."

"Yeah, I wanted to ask about that. I mean, I get the dating thing. Some parents are really crazy about it. But you can't even hang out with Mary Agnes, or somebody like that?"

"Of course not," I say, raising my eyebrows, pretending this is something scandalous. "She would corrupt me!"

"Mary Agnes? She couldn't corrupt anybody. She's like a parent's dream. Nomura, too. He's, like, a kid created by parents in a lab."

"Oh, but she's very nice. She's been very good to me."

"I know. I like her, too. But you know what I mean, right?"

"I have no idea what you mean." But I smile, and he understands me. "Anyway, Haitian parents are a little bit too strict, it's true. They think that if their children never see anybody outside the family, nothing can hurt them. But some things, even family cannot protect you from."

"Was your mother strict, when you lived in Haiti?"

He takes me by surprise with this. I do not know what to say. "Yes, she was strict, my mother."

"We don't have to talk about it," he says. "Not if you don't want to."

"No, it's okay, it's just—"

Then Jou Jou saves me. The driver's-side door swings open. "Here we are!" he says, carrying three foil-wrapped bundles and passing two back to Alex and me. As we open them, the thick, rich smell of goat meat fills the whole van. I pull out a big ball of hot, flaky dough and dip it into the mixture of goat meat, potatoes, and delicious sauce.

"You like it, yes?" I ask Alex after he tries his first bite. The meat, stringy but tender, is in perfect balance with the flaky, buttery bread.

"It's great," he says. "It's like a West Indian burrito. Perfect for a cold day like this."

"*Exactement.* Although we do not really have many cold days in the West Indies."

"So how was Trini-Daddy?" I ask Jou Jou. The old man is a favorite of ours, kind and welcoming.

"Good, good," he says. "Askin' about you, said to say hello to my 'ugly little sister.' "

"Oh, shut up," I say. But Alex is laughing, and so is my idiot brother.

"You know, he's more of a believer than Uncle," Jou Jou says, driving back toward Church Avenue. "He say he is very glad that I spread the word, the gospel, of the good Caribbean food. That good food make you a good Christian. He wants to make sure we will be a, how do you call it? A convert."

"Wow, he sounds worse than the priests at St. Chris's," Alex says.

"They are all the same," I say. "They try to change your life with a bit of bread." We all three laugh.

At the corner of Church and East Fifty-Second Street, Jou Jou pulls the car over again. He gets out and removes a large box from the back of the van behind our seats, and we walk into a store called Bull Bay One Stop Corner. The window advertises MEN AND LADIES WEAR, and in the windows, black-people mannequins model spring clothing, even though spring seems to be taking its time coming here to New York. Looking at those plastic people in their shorts and tank tops makes me miss home.

We open the door. "*Bonjour*, Guillaume!" cries Jou Jou before disappearing with the box down the stairs at the back of the store. Alex cranes his neck to see where my brother is going.

"Hallo, Bijou, and how are you today?" asks Monsieur Guillaume, the kind, gentle old Haitian man who lets Rara Gran Bwa practice in the basement underneath his shop. Sitting behind the button-operated cash register, he strokes his beard and smiles at me, ignoring Alex for the present. He's wearing an old blue sweatshirt; a purple birthmark sits on his left cheek like a coin; and his large, round eyeglasses are held together with duct tape.

"*Bonjour*, Monsieur Guillaume," I say. He leans forward, and I kiss him on both cheeks.

"Now that you have come to visit me, I can call my day complete, child. I can go home and eat my dinner in peace."

"*Merci*, Monsieur Guillaume." I feel color in my cheeks and am glad my skin doesn't give the secret away so easily.

Symphony music plays through a small black radio on a shelf behind Monsieur Guillaume's head. "And who is your friend, Bijou?" he asks. "A schoolmate?"

"This is Alex. He goes to St. Christopher's, the boys school."

"Ah, *Saint Christophe*," Monsieur Guillaume says, smiling like Buddha. "A very good saint for our people. He protect the traveling people, the people with the *hard* journey. So, Alex, you come to see the music today, have you?"

He shakes Alex's hand. The old man's grip looks strong.

"I don't know what I'm seeing, exactly," Alex says.

"Well, at least you're honest about it, young man." Guillaume chuckles.

"Have they started yet?" Bijou asks.

"They playing right now. Can't you hear them?"

He reaches back to turn down the radio, and I hear the rumbling Haitian drums coming through the floor, through my legs and toes, like some ancient machinery deep in the heart of the building.

"Come on, let's go," I say, taking Alex by the hand before realizing I've done so.

"Enjoy, children, enjoy God's music," Monsieur Guillaume says, who raises his eyebrows. I should not have reached for Alex's hand in front of him. Even if this behavior does not seem so bad to him, even though he does not know my aunt and uncle, he will still tease me without mercy. Is there any reason a Haitian girl exists except to be teased by her elders?

Alex and I take careful steps down the creaky, uneven steps, and I let go of his hand to place mine against the wall for balance. A single, bare bulb lights the entire basement, and there mustn't be a radiator here, because it is at least ten degrees colder than it was upstairs in the shop. But it is all right. I have become used to freezing alive, everywhere I go. That is life here in Brooklyn.

Most of the band is already here, and they greet us with a chorus of kind words. Jou Jou is passing out bright orange Rara Gran Bwa T-shirts from the box he carries, and the musicians grab at them like children fighting over candy. They grin and joke as if they have no care in the world, fighting to get the XXL shirts that hang well past their belts. Fabian says, "Gentlemen, one at a time!" but he is laughing, enjoying the band's playtime. Jou Jou tells me some of these boys have been away from their real families for so long that Fabian has become like their father. He cooks meals for them, counsels them when they are having troubles, even sometimes does their laundry. Other than Fabian, I do not know any of them well yet, but I love them for the way they have helped Jou Jou make Brooklyn a home. I can see that they truly care for him and that he has found more of a home in Rara Gran Bwa than he will ever have with Pierre and Marie Claire.

But today, while the band members are as kind and openhearted to Jou Jou and me as ever, it is Alex who is getting the special reception. The band members look at this white boy in a Flatbush basement as if he is an exotic animal.

Alex does not know what to do with the attention. He looks to me from the center of the room, the color rising to his face as always, with a look that says "help!" I have to laugh a little, looking at him here, surrounded by Rara Gran Bwa. I am sure that when Alex imagined the "date" we are supposed to be having, he never pictured this, being surrounded by a dozen tall black men with dreadlocks and drums. But now that he's here, in the Haitian world, there's no escape.

It will change him, whether he likes it or not.

 16

A Drum of My Own,
Then Something Better

Alex, come over here," Jou Jou says, his voice rising above the music. Rara Gran Bwa has been going full swing for fifteen minutes. The whole band is a blur of movement. I've never seen or heard anything like it. I can't keep my eyes off the drummers slapping those driving rhythms against the drumheads.

I glance at Bijou, who nods in her brother's direction, urging me forward. I walk to where Jou Jou is playing a repeating pattern on the rada: *bim-bap, bim-bap, bim-bim-bim-bap.*

"You try it!" Jou Jou yells.

"Really?" I ask.

"Come on, do it!"

Fabian, the older guy from the park, seems to approve. Jou Jou holds the head of the drum toward me, demonstrating how to strike it with a flat palm. "This, we call a slap," he says. Then, stopping the sound with his palm fully in the drum's center, "And this, we call 'bass.'" And finally, pinging out a higher tone on the drumhead's edge, "This one here? We say 'rim.'"

Then he shifts the drum over a little bit and gestures: *Your turn.*

I hesitate at first, but then I give it a try. Why not? What have I got to lose? I share the drum with him, copying the rhythm he's playing in its simplest form, trying to make my hands do what his are. After a while, I get it, and Jou Jou starts drumming more playfully, complicated rhythms on top with a stick. I start to bounce along with him in time, letting myself get carried along the pulse of the band. Fabian and other bandmates yell in my direction. But amazingly, they're not telling me to shut up and get the heck back upstairs. They're urging me to play *louder.*

I've forgotten about Bijou for a minute or two—although, is it really possible to forget Bijou, for even an instant?—but here she is now, dancing in the center of the musicians, like the spirit has gotten hold of her, too. She holds her arms out to the side, like she's squeezing a giant rubber ball between her hands. Then she bends her knees just so, and, feet closely rooted to the ground, shakes her hips to the rhythm.

"Ayooo, Bijou!" Fabian yells out to her.

Jou Jou is smiling and laughing at his sister's awesome dancing, and he can barely play his rada. I can't help but laugh, too. Bijou catches my eye, then, teasing, shakes her hip in a lazy, slow motion, like sending a wink my way. Is she flirting with me? Regardless, the next thing I know, I lose my rhythm and can't get it back. She's distracting me on purpose, and I can see Fabian and Jou Jou laughing at me. Not fair! I have to concentrate to get back into the groove, and, somehow, I manage.

When the music finishes, Fabian bounds over to me and pats me on the back.

"How long you been playin' rada, young Alex?"

"I've . . . never played before," I say, of course.

"Noooo," he says. "Impossible." I can tell he's teasing, but not in a mean way.

"Nope. First time."

The other band members talk among themselves, exchanging high fives (when they do it, they don't look as cheesy as Rocky and Trevor do) and handshakes.

"You're good, Alex, really," Jou Jou says. "You ever play *any* kind of music before?"

"My sister's the musical one in our family. She plays cello, really well. But my mom can't carry a tune, and I think I got her musical genes. I tried to learn guitar last year, and it didn't go so well."

"Well, you don't need to carry a tune to play rada,"

Fabian says. "But that doesn't mean it an easy thing. And you, you pick it up right away."

"It's a simple rhythm," I say. "Isn't it?"

Fabian calls the band together into a circle, like he did in the park. Only this time, I'm in the circle, too.

........— ℓℓℓℓℓ —........

"Alex, that was so good," Bijou says, back in the van. "How did you know how to do that?"

"I . . . don't know." The truth is, nothing like that has ever happened to me in my life. Everything came so naturally, and I'm not the kind of guy who's a natural at *anything*. "It was like I didn't even have to try. I just . . . let it happen."

"That's what I'm *telling* you," Jou Jou says, although I think this is actually the first time he's told me. "Rara's not about 'knowing' or 'trying'—it's about letting the music inside you. Right?"

"I couldn't say. I'm no good at music," Bijou says. She moves a little closer to me on the backseat. We're almost touching. I can feel an electric pulse between her legs and mine, and also an aching in my hand bones, where my palms hit the drum's wooden rim again and again. So my entire body is vibrating with one sensation or another.

"You can dance, though," I say. "Really well." I don't blush. I don't look down.

"I love to dance. I always have." She jabs me playfully. "You have talent, Alex. You should do something with it."

"You think so?" If she's going to keep moving closer to me like this, I'll definitely "do something" with music. To be honest, I'd do anything Bijou tells me.

"Alex," Jou Jou says, holding out his rada to me. "I want you to have this."

"What? Your drum? For me?" I say. I don't grab for it. I don't even touch it, not yet. It doesn't seem right.

"But what will you play?" I ask.

"You think this the only rada I got, Alex? I have another like it at home. This one, well, it has your name on it." He pushes the drum toward me again, and this time, I take it.

"Seriously?"

"Think of it like a—how do you call it—a long-term loan." Jou Jou doesn't leave me any time to argue. He turns around in his seat, starts the van, and heads up Church Avenue, in the direction of my house.

"Can you show me?" I ask him. "Maybe teach me some things?"

"Yeah, man, I'll be glad to. Anytime."

"Is this really okay?" I whisper to Bijou. Then, even quieter, "Does he really have a second one?"

Bijou puts her hand over my ear, and shivers go down my back. My eyes bug out for a sec. She can't see me, thankfully, but Jou Jou steals a quick glance at us in the rearview mirror and smiles. "You think my brother would be without a drum in his hands for more than fifteen minutes?" Bijou says. "This one's for you. Take it."

Jou Jou takes a left from Church Avenue onto Rugby Road. "This way?" he asks. A couple of people try to wave down the dollar van, but Jou Jou ignores them. "Next time," he chuckles.

"Yep, keep going another four blocks," I say. Ack, I can't believe I'm almost home. I don't want this to end. I wish I could stay in the backseat with Bijou forever.

As we get closer, I start to think about how I'm going to say good-bye to Bijou. When I saw her kiss Monsieur Guillaume in the shop, I had to admit once and for all that Nomura was right. The kiss-on-each-cheek custom is exactly that: a custom. Bijou did it as readily with the old man today as she did with me last week. So, I'm preparing myself for that again, and hopefully I won't bump heads with her and be all awkward about it.

"Keep going this way?" Jou Jou asks. We are at Rugby Road and Cortelyou, almost on my block. For the first time, I notice how different my neighborhood is from Church and Rogers, where we were ten minutes ago. Here, the houses are bigger and set apart, with front porches and spacious backyards.

Suddenly, I realize that I don't want them to drop me off right in front of the house. My mom might be home now, and I didn't exactly tell her where I was going today. "Oh, hey, I need to get something for my mom at the bakery," I say, nodding toward Steve's, on the corner. "Would you mind letting me off here?"

"No problem," Jou Jou says, pulling the van over by a fire hydrant.

Darn, this date is ending even sooner than I'd realized. There's only so much you can prepare. "Bijou, can we do this again sometime?" I ask. "Sometime soon?"

"Yes, I would like that," she says. "Very much."

"Thank you, Bijou." I suddenly realize how hot I am, maybe flushed still, from the drumming. Or from other things.

"For what?" she asks.

"For today. For . . . everything." I pick up the drum and get ready to leave. "Jou Jou, thank you *so much* for the rada. I'll take really good care of it."

"You're welcome, man. Call me, and I'll give you some things to work on."

"Cool, I'll do that."

Then I lean in for the kiss on the cheek. Now that I know what I'm doing, it feels a little more natural. We don't bump heads, anyway. I don't try to linger or make the moment last any longer than she wants; after all, Jou Jou is right there—he can see everything. But I try to freeze the memory in my brain, so I can hold on to that almond-flower smell of Bijou's skin as long as possible. It's got to last me until the next time I see her, after all.

17

New, Crazy Powers

My favorite part of any superhero movie is what the superhero does after he figures out for the first time that he has all these new, crazy powers. With a look of shock and wonder on his face, he flies around the city late at night, jumping from building to building, testing the limits of what he can do while trying not to clobber any innocent bystanders. Like a young deer that can barely stand on its legs one minute and is sprinting through grassy fields the next, the superhero takes some falls, too. Young Superman is going to lose his concentration when he encounters mid-air turbulence, and Spidey's going to bang into some brick walls before saving himself with his brand-new web shooter. But whatever minor suffering he experiences along the way, the superhero's first trip out into the world after his transformation, after he has become his new self, is a total blast. You can see the joy, the awesome new confidence, all over his face.

"What are *you* smirking at?" Rocky asks me when I pass him in the hall, and I immediately duck into the bathroom so I can check myself out in the mirror. Of course, whatever smirk Rocky saw is long gone, but I need to remember not to reveal too much, at least not to any St. Chris supervillains. If I slam into a brick wall, I don't have a web shooter to save myself.

During science, first period, Mr. Chamberlain is droning on about animal cell anatomy. But the only cells I'm interested in are the ones in my brain that hold the memories of my time with Bijou. I use these cells, which, next to Nomura, are pretty much my best friends right now, to replay everything that happened yesterday. I fast-forward, rewind, and slo-mo each moment so many times that I'm worried the images will start to dissolve at the edges, like an old photo worn thin from too much touching. Part of me wants to distract myself with other thoughts, to keep the memories from blurring until I don't recognize them anymore, but I can't help myself; I need to keep on remembering.

Ira breaks the spell, leaning over his desk while Chamberlain is droning on and on. "I hear you had yourself a big day yesterday," he whispers. He's weirdly out of breath.

How does he know? I haven't even talked to Nomura yet. "Tell me about it," he says.

"Later," I say.

"Come on, dude. Tell me. Did you . . . get some?"

"*Get some?*" I whisper. "Keep your voice down."

"Did you . . . you know, did anything *happen*?"

"Nothing I'm gonna tell *you* about," I say, turning stiffly away from him as if I'm actually paying attention to Chamberlain.

"Bijou is so . . ." Ira looks so . . . sad, like he did at the dance when gushing about Jenna Minaya. It's like he's forcing himself to say the words but doesn't get their actual meaning. "So totally hot."

I can't hide my expression of, I don't know . . . is it outright disgust? Doesn't Ira know not to talk about someone I care about like this? We're not talking about Jenna Minaya here. We're talking about *Bijou Doucet*. "Grow up, already."

"I am grown up, jerk." His voice has a bitter edge I've never heard before. He turns away. Suddenly, the two of us are Mr. Chamberlain's most attentive students. "I'll find out soon enough, anyway."

"What are you going to do, make a video about it?" Why am I being so mean to him? I can't help it, somehow.

"Shut up, Alex." He looks hurt.

"Sorry, man, that was harsh," I say.

But am I really that sorry?

I've never heard Ira talk about *getting some*, but maybe that's because none of us has *ever* gotten any. Then I look at Ira's messy hair and untucked shirt, and I wonder why Nomura and I ever befriended him in the first place. We were only third graders when we started hanging out, and Ira's quirks were funny back then, not annoying. But now, as he strains so desperately to be cool, to keep up, he's not so amusing anymore. I abandon the conversation and pretend to take notes on membranes and centrosomes.

But at lunch, there Ira still is, a glutton for punishment as usual, tagging along as Nomura and I grab food upstairs. We're trading bites of a couple of the orange Hostess cupcakes Ira brought to school and chatting about nothing in particular—you can't really talk about anything interesting when Ira's around, and Nomura gets that, knows that I'll tell him stuff when I'm ready to tell him stuff—when I get a text from Mary Agnes: "I hear things went well yesterday, congrats. Next step: group date. Movie?"

"Who from?" Nomura asks.

"Mary Agnes."

"Mary Agnes? What's she say?" Ira asks, looking over my shoulder and reading the text before I can shield it from him. "Oh right, the movie."

"Dude, knock it off," I say, pushing him away.

"What?" he says, superoffended.

"This isn't about you, okay? You're . . . not invited."

Nomura gives me a look: *Simmer down, man.* I don't know what's gotten into me, but I can't help it. Ira's driving me nuts.

"I am too. Mari and I are the ones who thought it up," Ira says, taking the last bite of cupcake. "I was invited before you even knew it existed. I even picked the movie." He walks away like a shamed dog, the hurt and pain so close to the surface I swear he's about to cry.

"You're being a little intense, man," Nomura says once he's gone.

"I know. But he's really been getting on my nerves lately. I don't have any patience for him anymore." I ball up my lunch bag and throw it in the trash.

"Maybe you should take it a little easier on him anyway, though. I mean, we've been friends for a long time. It should count for something."

"You're right. I know you're right." Sometimes it's not about what Nomura is actually saying; it's just that his voice is the sonic equivalent of wisdom and calm, and to do anything but submit to it is pointless.

Still, I change the subject. "So, let me guess. You already know more about this movie plan than I do, huh?"

"Probably, yeah. Mary Agnes won't stop texting me. She's even called me three times since you went on your little drum date with Bijou." Ah, so even Nomura knows there were drums involved.

"She could easily text *me*. Or call."

"Exactly. She's *choosing* to call me instead."

"Why?"

"Mary Agnes is a big-time matchmaker. And not just for you and Bijou."

"What do you mean? Like, she's using me and Bijou to get to you?" Nomura nods. "That's weird," I say.

"I guess it is a little strange. She's fundamentally a nice person, though."

"So you can go with it for a little bit longer? Help me out and do this group-date thing?"

"Sure."

"Cool." I resist the urge to tease him; does he like Mary Agnes back? Two weeks ago, if I had thought there was even a chance of that, I would have let him have it. But now, I have too much at stake, so I don't really care whether Nomura's doing this for me, for him, or both. All I care is that he's doing it at all. "One thing, though. What about the fact that Bijou can't go out with friends unless her brother's around?"

Nomura shrugs. "Mary Agnes says they've got that all figured out."

"Really? How?"

"I'm not sure, exactly."

"Well, we'll find out soon enough, I guess."

It's hard to imagine that having that particular

problem "figured out" involves Bijou bringing Jou Jou along. I mean, would she really do that, have him sit behind a row of kids six years younger than him? He's a cool guy, but he wouldn't want to go to a movie with a bunch of kids. Hopefully she's got another idea.

"Anyway, it's gonna be that movie *Terror Lake*," Nomura continues.

"Oh no. Is this Ira's idea of revenge?" He and Nomura both know I hate scary movies (Ira loves them, naturally), and I've seen the poster for this one: A gnarled hand clutching a dagger breaks the surface of a lake. In the background, the windows of a tiny cabin glow eerily. Perfect.

"I don't know. Probably."

"Can we change it? You know how I get."

"They've already picked a showtime at the Pavilion and everything."

He gives me a sympathetic look, knowing I've done everything in my power to avoid scary movies since I was eight, when I watched *A Nightmare on Elm Street* with Dolly. "What are you doing? Are you following me?" she asked as I followed her downstairs to the kitchen, too afraid to stay in the TV room by myself. I told her I was too cold up there, that I wanted to make the hot chocolate *my* way, and whatever else I could think of off the top of my head, but she didn't believe me. "It's only a movie, fraidy-cat."

Fraidy-cat is not the image I'm going for. But Nomura,

who's no fan of scary movies himself, claims they're the best choice for dates. "It's been scientifically proven," he says. "Scary movies are better."

"What do you mean?" I say.

"Research says that the most pleasant moments of a particular event may also be the most fearful."

"English. Speak English."

"Fear makes the heart rate quicken."

"Believe me, so does being with a girl."

"Exactly. You're both nervous about the date and nervous about the movie. And that brings you together. You hold hands. You put your arm around her. You do your thing."

"Oh, please. Just like that?"

"Just like that."

"And you know this . . . how?"

"From my own experience as a lady-killer and all-around stud. Duh." Nomura scooches up next to me and jokingly demonstrates his arm technique. "It's easy. Pretend you're about to yawn, like this." Exaggerating extreme fatigue, he opens his mouth so wide I can see half his lunch. I'm so distracted by the over-the-top yawn parody that I don't notice his arm around my shoulder until it's already there. "Not bad, not bad." Then he nuzzles me, all moony-eyed.

"Quit it, man," I say, laughing.

"Now *this* is scary," Rocky says, appearing out of

nowhere. "Are you guys just practicing, or are you actually in love?"

"Tough call," Trevor says, cracking up. "But that's as close as Schrader's ever going to get to scoring."

"What are you guys gonna go see, anyway?" Rocky asks. *"Diary of a Wimpy Kid?* Or would that be a little too auto-biographical?"

Trevor chuckles. We don't say anything, which is usually the best way to handle the two of them.

"Hey, that's an idea," Trevor says. "You guys could act out a chick flick like that for Musicale. Everybody'll *love* that!"

"Nice, dude," Rocky says. And . . . it's high-five time.

"Oh, and Alex, after you finish your popcorn? Enjoy the dessert." Rocky strolls away. Trevor, as always, follows.

"What do you mean, 'dessert'?" I ask.

Nomura jabs me, a reminder I should have stayed quiet. He's more disciplined than I am.

"You know," Rocky says. "Everybody likes a little taste of brown sugar."

"What?" I say. Another jab from Nomura.

"Your little girlfriend. I'll bet she tastes like brown sugar."

"You did not just say that." What would all the St. Cat's girls say if I'd gotten a recording of *this* and put it up on the Web?

"Oh, I did, Alex," Rocky says. "I did."

I turn to Trevor. "Trevor, I was wondering if you'd noticed: your girlfriend's black, too."

"Uhh, yeah, I think I noticed that," Trevor says.

"And you're cool with him talking about another black girl like that?"

"Don't pee in your pants, dude. I take it as a compliment."

Then Rocky gives me a light shove against my locker. "You're a lucky guy, Schrader, getting a date with a girl like that. But you've got to be careful. After all, you're a U.S. citizen, don't forget. Next thing you know, she'll try to marry you so she can stay in the country."

"That is the stupidest thing I've ever heard," I say. "Even if she was like that, Bijou doesn't need to do that to stay in the country. She's got plenty of family here."

"You're right, I'm getting ahead of myself. Nobody's marrying anybody here. There's no way you're even getting to first base, much less walking down the aisle. I must have forgotten who I was talking to."

I'll tell you who you're talking to, Rocky. You're talking to the guy who's going to get the girl he likes.

"Maybe *I'll* marry her, man," Trevor says. "She's supercute."

Barf. Just when I think these guys can't sink any lower, they do. I wish I could come up with an awesome response, but as I've shown again and again, I'm not exactly the Comeback Kid. All I can manage is a disgusted sneer.

"What about Jenna?" Rocky asks, playing along.

"Meh, we're together, but we're not *together* together, you know?" He laughs. "Jenna's a babe. But Bijou's so much more . . . exotic."

"Right? Gotta love that accent." Rocky clucks his tongue. So gross.

"Schrader, if Bijou ever winds up entering the twenty-first century and getting herself a cell phone," Trevor asks, "you'll be a bro and give me her number, right? I'd like to give her a buzz sometime."

Yeah, that'll happen, Trevor.

The two idiots strut away, laughing and shoving each other. I wish Ira were around with his stupid video cam; this little scene would make for *excellent* viewing. Angela and Jenna aren't what I'd call brilliant judges of moral character, but they should get a chance to see who their boyfriends really are, shouldn't they? Any girl with half a brain would bail on them in a nanosecond.

I've seen it again and again, though, and it's impossible to ignore: the supposedly "hottest" girls like the jerkiest guys. All I can do is hope and pray that Bijou, the cutest and coolest girl of them all, turns out to be different.

.... ℓℓℓℓℓ ....

Speaking of Bijou, it's sure been hard to get in touch with her since the date. She seriously must be the only person in the St. Cathopher's universe to not have a phone. I've been losing my mind; I really, really want to talk to her. Luckily, Mary Agnes, innovative as usual, has come up with a solution.

During school hours, I can send a text to Mary Agnes, and she'll pass it on to Bijou. In turn, Bijou can use Mary Agnes's phone to text me. Of course, this means that Bijou's self-appointed best friend knows every single thought, every emotion that passes between us, but for now, it's a price I'm willing to pay.

"Put 'FOR B' at the beginning, and I won't read those ones," Mary Agnes said.

Yeah, right.

So Bijou and I have kept things pretty basic. I've asked her how things are going, how her day went, stuff like that. And her responses have been pretty, let's say, nonspecific. I mean, I know it's her, not Mary Agnes, writing them. There have been references to Jou Jou, to Rara Gran Bwa, to her aunt and uncle. But if I'm going to have so few opportunities to actually hang out in public with the girl I like, I'm going to have to find a way to get to know her, a way for her to get to know me, *without* Mary Agnes having access to our private feelings.

So I've come up with something: the Trini-Daddy's tree—an idea so old-school, so simple, I can't believe it took me this long to figure it out. But now that I have, I love it. It totally avoids detection by anybody but me and Bijou, and while it's almost as labor-intensive as the Pony Express, it's also pretty fun.

Yesterday, I sent Bijou a text at Mary Agnes's number that said, "Something for U. Trini-Daddy's Tree. Look after school today." That was it! And the genius part is that Trini-Daddy's isn't listed on Google *or* through 411. I checked, and unless you live in Flatbush and walk by the place every day—which, with the sole exception of Bijou, nobody from either St. Chris's or St. Cat's ever does—it's virtually impossible to trace. I wrote her this letter, where I put everything I've been thinking since the day we met into words. Am I nuts?

Nomura thinks so, that I'm saying too much, too soon, but I don't care. If I don't tell her this stuff, I'm going to go loony, and I'm no good to anyone completely off my rocker. So I just went for it, speeding through the note in about seven minutes, and now I can barely remember a word of it. I hope I didn't say anything completely crazy.

18

Our Own Gran Bwa

I walk down Flatbush Avenue, following Alex's instructions exactly. The note is right where he said it would be, stuffed into a small knot in the tree outside Trini-Daddy's. I don't know about this crazy boy, leaving me notes in bushes and trees. What is he going to say? There is a part of me that is excited, and flattered, but a bigger part of me that is terrified of anyone seeing me. Especially my uncle, although yes, I do know that Tonton Pierre is not following me around, looking at everything I do. It only feels that way.

I look at the tree, which is a very tall one, at least twenty-five feet, impressive for a sidewalk in the middle of a busy city. Did Alex realize that he was directing me to our own Gran Bwa? The tree's branches spread wide, like open arms, like a giant conductor that organizes the honking car horns, the throaty yells of the street, into a driving, powerful rhythm.

How strange it must look for a girl to pull paper out of a tree. And how embarrassing. But Alex was smart about one thing: this section of Flatbush Avenue is as busy as it gets. I could be walking down the street with half my clothes off in the middle of winter, and no one would be bothered. These New York people, they keep their eyes in front of them at all times and do not bother with the doings of others.

I look in both directions, pull the note out, then quickly enter the stream of walking traffic.

Dear Bijou,

Please God, I hope it's you, Bijou, reading this, and not some creep on the street. (If this is a creep on the street, you should put this letter down right now because it's not for you. It belongs to me, and it belongs to Bijou, but anybody else? Well, it's none of your business, so put it back where it belongs so Bijou can find it the way she's meant to.)

Anyway, Bijou, did I ever tell you about the first time I saw you? I'm pretty sure you couldn't, or didn't, see me, but I saw you. And you know how in movies, you hear people say things like "my heart stopped" or "time stopped" or "love hit me like an arrow"? Well, I always thought that was a bunch of junk, but when I first saw you at Peas n' Pickles with Mary Agnes, it was exactly like that. Like my life had changed in a millisecond, and I would never be the same.

I felt different, as in like the person I was before but bigger and better. I felt like, and I don't mean this to sound strange, but I felt like I was meant to know you, that somehow you were going to be a part of my life. Don't ask me how, but I knew it.

It's not because you're pretty. I mean, you're really, really, really pretty, prettier than any other girl I've ever seen, but it's not like that at all. It's more like there was something about you that made me think we were meant to get to know each other better. (A look in your eyes? An expression? I honestly don't know for sure.) And not just to be a "couple," but really, truly get to know each other. And I knew I needed to do whatever I could to get to meet you.

I hope that doesn't sound weird, but it's the truth!

If you want to write me back, and I hope you do, you can leave a letter for me right here in this tree.

Your friend,

Alex

P.S. I'm seeing you for the movie Saturday, right? I hope so....

He is not holding *anything* back, is he? I look up and down the street, making sure that no one I know can see me. If Alex is trying to make me blush as badly as he does, he is succeeding, and even my complexion is not able to hide it. This is a sweet boy I have met, a very sweet one.

Which is why I have so many different feelings as I read the letter, then read it a second time, taking care not to bump into anyone on the crowded sidewalk. Have I ever been so excited to see someone? I don't think so! Thinking about this sweet, blushing boy, it gives me gooseflesh.

But another part of me feels guilty, so guilty and wrong, for lying to Pierre and Marie Claire.

It took nearly an hour of pleading, almost begging, before they would allow me to do what they *think* I am going to do on Saturday afternoon: spend it with Maricel and Mary Agnes at Mary Agnes's house. "Even the suggestion is outrageous!" was the first thing Tonton Pierre said when I brought up the idea of spending only a few hours with a couple of friends from school.

I did do one thing right, though: I brought it up with Marie Claire first. And I made sure to tell her all about the girls, who had been "so supportive and kind" to me during these first months in America.

"Pierre, this is what American girls do: they spend time together," Marie Claire said only a few minutes later, trying to build up my case to Uncle. "They get to know each other."

"They cannot 'get to know each other' in school?"

In the end, though, she convinced him, on the condition

that he would speak to Mary Agnes's mother beforehand, and that he would have the phone number and address of the Bradys' house in Park Slope, only a couple of miles from Flatbush. (He even wanted to go by the Bradys' house and look at it, but we talked him out of it, thank God.) Finally, he made me swear that I would be seeing *only* the two girls and that I would not leave Mary Agnes's house during the entire time I was to be there, under any circumstances.

Uh-oh. I did swear to it. I lied to the face of my mother's brother. To see a boy! I can only pray that everything goes exactly as planned, because if I get caught, that will be the end.

Can Mary Agnes really be right, that we can go out to the movie without her mother noticing? According to Mary Agnes, every Saturday afternoon, no exceptions, her mother leaves at 2 p.m. and does not return until five. The movie begins at two thirty and will end before four thirty. That gives us a few minutes to say good-bye to the boys before returning to Mary Agnes's house, which is only three blocks from the theater. Then my uncle will pick me up at exactly six o'clock. He is never late.

So, yes, a part of me is so frightened that some small detail in our plan will go wrong. But there is another part of me, almost as big, that doesn't care at all, that wants to tell Tonton Pierre, "You are not my father, and you are not the boss of me!"

And this, too: now that I am in America, is it so wrong that I should be allowed to enjoy the simple things that other American kids do? It is so hard being here, so far away from those I truly do consider family—Maman and Gran-Papa—that I feel I should be able to do what I want. I have lost so much; shouldn't I be allowed to have even a little fun? I think so.

19

No Drumming at the Table

What the heck *is* that ugly thing?" Dolly asks. We're helping Mom get dinner ready in the kitchen, and it's the first time either one of them has laid eyes on my new drum, which I told them I borrowed from Mr. Sinclair, the goofy, mustachioed music teacher who actually does have a bunch of weird bongos and other things lying around his office. I'm sitting on a stool and giving them a sample of my flashy new skills.

"It's called a rada," I say. "Sorry it's not as beautiful as your impossibly perfect *cello*." And it's true that there couldn't have been more of a contrast between the rada—with its rough, wooden sides; crude pegs; and worn-down, sweat-stained cow-skin head—and Dolly's finely polished, two-thousand-dollar cello, which my mom had to buy on layaway. "But I'm going to be better on this drum than you'll ever be on that stuck-up old thing."

"Dream on, Alex."

The truth is, of course, I'm a total beginner on this drum, and will be for a long, long time. But there is a feeling I get when I play the rada, when I practice my patterns, that I can do anything, be anything. That I can be a good musician one day, or talk to a girl who's as beautiful and cool and mysterious as Bijou without feeling like I'm going to have a panic attack. I saw Bijou watch me while I was playing. She wasn't looking at me like I was some pest who couldn't take no for an answer. She was looking at me like I was someone worth getting to know.

"Alex, you know I support you taking an interest in something," Mom says.

"I'm gonna play it for Musicale this year," I say, the thought occurring to me at exactly the same moment the words are coming out of my mouth. It's a cool idea, though. Musicale is a big deal at St. Cathopher's, an open call for anybody in fifth grade and above. Everybody from both schools is required to watch, and the show usually lasts almost three hours. But I've never been able to sign up, because I've never been good at anything. Until now.

"That's wonderful, Alex," Mom says. "I'm looking forward to hearing you play some more. But until dinner's over, please put the drum—"

"It's called a rada," I say. Dolly giggles.

"Sorry, please put the *rada* away until dinner's over."

"Yeah, no rada-ing at the table, bro." Dolly smirks.

This is the first time the three of us have had a meal together in weeks. We're preparing salmon steaks marinated in soy, ginger, and garlic, and Mom gets a small cut on her right thumb while slicing spring onions.

"Ack," she says. "I need to run up and get a Band-Aid. Can you guys take over here?"

We can, and we do. I squeeze lemon juice into the marinade, and Dolly makes a salad.

"So, is this, like, revenge against me playing the cello all these years?" Dolly asks. "Or are you trying to work your way into a certain Haitian girl's good graces?"

God, I'm an idiot. Of course Dolly was going to put two and two together. "But don't tell Mom, okay?" I whisper.

"I won't, I won't. But you should really be more careful. Mom's no fool." Dolly throws a handful of chopped carrots into the salad bowl and starts working on the dressing, whisking oil and vinegar, mustard, and honey in a small bowl. "I have to say, though, you do sound pretty good on that thing, for just a few days." And she looks genuinely impressed. I've never been good at *anything* before, really, and the whole family knows it.

"Thanks," I say. And unable to resist, "If my drumming keeps you up, remember the five hundred million mornings your cello has woken me up at the crack of dawn."

"That drum is *so* much louder than my cello." She puts a stainless-steel pan on the grill, lights the flame underneath, and drizzles some olive oil on the pan's hot surface.

"Don't be so sure about that. That oversize ukelele can shake the picture frames off the walls."

"So, how's it going with her, anyway?" She lowers her voice. "Are you guys a couple yet?"

Dolly plops three chunks of salmon steak on the pan. They pop and sizzle. She tends to them with a metal spatula and waits for my answer.

"Definitely just friends. I don't really know how to, you know, make it more than that."

"All your friends are trying to get you to make your move, right? Be the big stud?"

"I don't know. Kind of, I guess." I decide to take a risk and trust my sister. She is, after all, older and supposedly wiser. She's had a boyfriend. Just nerdy Jerome, a violinist with bad acne and a jittery, nervous laugh, but still. "Dolly, is she going to *want* me to? You know, to make a move?"

"Well, probably, yeah. But it doesn't have to be anything major. The important thing is that you *show* her that you like her. And you do that by doing what comes naturally, not by pretending to yawn so you can get your arm around her."

Okay, so my sister's advice is the exact opposite of Nomura's. But which one of them is right?

I sidestep the question for now. "How would I 'make a move' anyway? We're not even allowed to be alone together for a single minute."

"Strict parents, huh?"

"It's her aunt and uncle, and it's way beyond strict. It's like she's completely outlawed from having contact with not just boys, but even girls her own age. It's completely forbidden."

"Wow, that's pretty old-school. Can you imagine Mom trying to control us like that, every moment of our lives? Did they just move here or something?"

"They've been here for thirty years. I don't think they're going to change."

"Well, in that case, maybe you'll have to . . . get creative."

"I already have."

"Umm, *bad* idea," Mom says, walking into the kitchen and applying some pressure to her bandaged finger. How much of our conversation did she hear? "Whoever we're talking about here? Her family has rules, and they need to be respected."

"Even if they were written in the Middle Ages?" Dolly says.

Mom ignores the comment. "Just like our family's rules need to be respected."

Exactly, like rules about me hanging out in a dollar van, or going to a rara jam session after dark in Prospect Park when I told her I was studying with Nomura.

"What are our family's rules, exactly?" I ask.

"Yeah, Mom," Dolly says, smiling. "What are they?"

"Rule number one: honesty," Mom says, definitely *not*

smiling. "If you guys follow *that* rule, then we don't really need many others."

"Okay," Dolly and I say. Dolly gives me a look, like *Yikes.*

We set the table and put down the food in silence, and I'm hoping Mom won't start asking questions that actually put "rule number one" to the test. But no such luck.

Before we've even taken our first bite, Mom says, "Alex, do you want to tell me who you and Dolly were talking about, and what exactly your relationship with her is?" Mom has that look of trying to control her emotions after hearing something that has really bowled her over. But is it really so shocking that I'm interested in a girl? I'm in seventh grade, after all.

Without any other options (or time to think of any), I go ahead and tell her everything I know about Bijou. She's from Haiti, she's been here less than three months, she lives with her superstrict uncle, and she has a brother who's an awesome drummer.

"That's all you know?" Dolly laughs. "Maybe you should try asking her a question or two sometime."

"Dahlia, be nice," Mom says.

"You think I don't want to? I'd love to know more about her, but it's hard. I'm really supposed to start firing away with superpersonal questions with everyone hovering around us all the time?"

"These Haitian parents are heavily into supervision," Dolly says.

"So am I," Mom says, looking stern. And then, to me, "Alex, you really don't know what happened to her—wait, what's her name again?"

"Bijou."

"Very pretty. You don't know anything about what happened to her family during the earthquake?"

"That was three years ago."

"That might seem like a long time to you, but it's really not. Did she lose anyone? Her mom or dad?"

"I don't think so. She talks about her mom sometimes, and I think her dad's been . . . out of the picture for a while now."

Mom shrugs and gives a short laugh. She knows a little something about out-of-the-picture dads. "So why did she move here, then?"

"I don't know." I have to admit, in all this time, I hadn't really thought about it before. It's been hard enough to keep up with Bijou in the present, much less subject her to nosy questions about her past.

"Maybe you should find out," Dolly says, as if I needed to feel any stupider right now.

"Dahlia, enough," Mom says. "Alex, do you know how Bijou lived in Haiti? Was her family in the camps?"

"I think she lived in a house."

"Really?"

"They used to have servants, before the earthquake. I think they might have been rich or something."

"Are you sure about that, Alex? I don't think there are very many people in Haiti who have, or who ever had, servants."

"Mom, you've never even been to Haiti. Not everybody there is poor, no matter what you see on the news."

"Alex, please don't use that tone with me."

"I'm sorry. I just don't see why it's such a big deal that I was with somebody who happened to be in an earthquake."

"It was more than just any old earthquake, and I think you know that. What I'm trying to say is, a young girl, with everything she's been through, the complexity of her emotions must be absolutely overwhelming. She may have post-traumatic stress disorder." *Post-traumatic stress disorder.* Okay, that's something I'm going to need to look up. "Even if Bijou was lucky enough to avoid any major tragedy during the quake, moving to a new country, being so far away from her mother for the first time, it's . . . a lot."

"But she seems fine to me." I almost said, *She seems fine* with *me.*

"She might appear fine on the outside, but believe me, with what she's been through, below the surface, things are bound to be way more complicated."

"So I shouldn't be friends with her because her life's been hard?"

"No, Alex. And must you turn this into an argument?

I am not saying you shouldn't, or can't, spend time with her. But I *am* saying that you should be aware of her circumstances. She has a lot on her plate right now, and it might be a lot for a boy your age to take in."

"I'm old enough, Mom. I understand things."

Dolly rolls her eyes, and I remind myself to get her back for that as soon as Mom's out of sight.

"Alex, just promise to talk to me, even if it's awkward, okay?" Yeah, like that's going to happen; I'm going to talk to my mom about what's happening between me and the *first girl I've ever liked.* "Keep me posted on how things go with her?"

"You never make me tell you about what it's like when I hang out with Nomura, or Ira. Why is Bijou any different?"

"Because she's a girl, you dummy," Dolly says, shaking her head. I know I'm being ridiculous, but aren't I allowed to keep this stuff private?

"I have to report on my activities all of a sudden, because I like a girl?"

"You don't have to be so dramatic," Mom says. "But if you put it that way, Alex, you're still young enough that I should know who you're with after school. If you say you're studying with Nomura, you'd better be studying with Nomura."

Wait, does she know I've already thrown a couple of half truths her way? Knowing that my agro approach to this conversation has backfired badly, I say, "Okay, Mom," hoping this'll be enough to end it.

"I can tolerate a lot from you kids, but I won't put up with lying. Honesty is everything to me."

"I get it, Mom. Promise."

But she's not done. Not quite yet. "And I still don't want you on Flatbush, or anywhere east of there, after dark."

She gives me an I-mean-business look, and I wonder whether or not I should mention that I was there the other day. Or that I'm about forty-five hours away from my first group date. I decide to keep it to myself for now. The Pavilion's in a "good" neighborhood, after all. So does Mom really need to know?

·····———eeee———·····

On Friday, I find another envelope in my locker. The same neat block letters, the same violent underlining.

What do you really know about her, anyway? She's lying to you. About everything. Better to dump her before you learn the truth.

I scan the hall. Mostly lower-schoolers. Like last time, I get the eerie sense that someone is watching me, that somebody, somewhere, is waiting around for me to open the note. Wouldn't that be where the satisfaction would come from in writing such a thing? Wouldn't the author want to see my reaction, see whether I got nervous, scared, or angry?

My first thought, of course, is that it's Rocky, Trevor, or both. *Whoever you are, I sure hope you feel good about yourself, Mr. Anonymous. I hope you're having the time of your life.*

20

Alex's "Move"

There he is, at last. I can see Alex on the corner, blowing his hands against the cold.

So far, everything has gone as planned. Tonton Pierre dropped me off at Mary Agnes's, with stern warnings, at one thirty, and her mother left at exactly 2 p.m. to get her Saturday spa treatment. "It's my weekend ritual," she said on her way out the door. She was expecting a laugh, but it didn't sound like a joke to me, so I just smiled.

Mary Agnes and Maricel are both wearing pink Converse shoes, jeans, and purple T-shirts. Part of me wishes they would tell me when they plan to match like twins, and another part of me thinks they look ridiculous and is glad I have my own outfit on. I wear a pair of light blue pants (not jeans, though) that Marie Claire gave me and a white Izod shirt. Honestly, I am just glad not to be wearing any polka dots.

"I can't wait to see John," Mary Agnes says, hugging herself. She means Nomura.

"You're too cute," Maricel says.

"Are you psyched to see Alex, Bijou?" Mary Agnes asks. "Things definitely seem to be moving along for you, right?"

"Shh," I say. "They'll hear us." I deliberately speed up so I won't have to answer. Yes, things are moving along, but that doesn't mean I want to talk about it. Americans share too much. Far too much.

"Hi. How are you?" Alex says, handing me a ticket for the movie. He is looking only at me, as if my friends, and his, do not exist.

"Fine," I say. "Good to see you. And . . . thank you for this."

"You're welcome." Alex takes half a step forward, then hesitates. I save him by kissing him on the cheek. Suddenly, everyone is hugging one another and trying their own version of the cheek kisses. "Ooh la la," Mary Agnes says. When Americans meet, I've noticed, they don't know what to do: kiss, hug, or shake hands? Even a simple hello can turn awkward.

"As long as I don't have to kiss Maricel," Ira says. "Ick."

"Right back at you," Maricel says.

With the greetings over, we hand our tickets to the usher and are directed upstairs. Maricel and Mary Agnes go to the bathroom and pull me along with them; the three boys go, too (into the men's room, I mean!). As soon as we're inside, Mary Agnes starts checking her makeup, even though she did that at home ten minutes ago. Maricel does, too, wondering aloud why she's doing so when Nomura and Alex are already "taken."

"You never know who you might run into," Mary Agnes says.

"No makeup?" Maricel asks me. I shake my head. I've never worn makeup in my life. Maman wouldn't allow it. But I do check my hair to be sure it's tucked neatly into its bun.

"She's so dark," Mary Agnes says. "She doesn't need makcup. Look how flawless her skin is."

I let the remark pass. If she doesn't think black women use makeup, she must be blind. And I'm not much darker than Maricel, who's got plenty of it on. Do I look "blacker" to Mary Agnes because I'm from Haiti? After all, Maricel's family is from the Dominican Republic, which is on the *same island* as my country.

"Okay, Bijou, John and Alex will probably try to make a move during the movie, so don't be surprised. Just . . . go with it."

"What is 'make a move'?" I ask. "You mean, like, kissing?" There is no way I'm going to let Alex kiss me. While surrounded by other people? No way. Kissing is something to be shared between two people, not a whole movie theater.

"Well, he'll probably start like this," Maricel says. She

stands next to me, leans back, yawns, and slowly drapes her arm over my shoulder before cracking up laughing.

"They pretend to be *tired* to get close to you?" I ask. "That doesn't sound like a compliment."

"It's because they're shy," Mary Agnes says. "It's kind of cute when you think about it."

"Don't I have any say in what happens?" I ask. "I'm not just something for him to do whatever he likes with."

"Just go with it, Bijou," Mary Agnes says. She sounds like one of the teachers. "It's the way things are done here."

The boys actually take longer to come out of the bathroom than we do, and Alex and Ira seem to be having some kind of disagreement.

"It's gone, see?" Ira says, showing him the screen on his video cam.

"It better be," Alex responds before putting a smile on for me.

The theater is dark and only about one-third full, and Alex and Nomura are whispering, trying to figure out where to sit. On the screen, a message tells us not to smoke, talk, or use cell phones. This should not be a problem. I still don't have a cell phone, I left my cigarettes at home (a bad joke, but I do try to entertain myself), and it's the boys talking, not me.

"Come on, man," Alex whispers to Ira, who wants to sit next to us. "Give us a *little* room." *Oh no, Alex, please. No kissing attempts, not here!*

"I like the aisle," Alex says, in a more "public" whisper, one loud enough for our group to hear, but not too loud to disturb those around us who have been seated for some time already.

"So do I," says Mary Agnes.

"We'll sit behind you guys. That okay with you, Bijou?" I nod. So embarrassing. If Alex does anything more than put his arm around my shoulder, I'll elbow him right in the belly, I swear it. No matter how much I like him.

"I get it, everybody wants *privacy*," Ira says, quite loudly.

"Shhh!" hisses someone from the middle of the theater.

"Settle down, Ira," whispers Nomura, who takes the seat between Mary Agnes and Maricel. Ira sits next to Alex.

"Great, I'm sitting next to my own sister," Ira says. "Next thing, Aunt Malinda's going to magically appear in my lap."

"Quiet, the trailers are starting," says Mary Agnes.

Alex sits back in his chair, gives me a glance and a quick, not-quite-comfortable smile. In the first preview, a handsome, boyish-looking man—not so different from an older Alex, really—is sitting cross-legged with a pretty white girl, eating cereal on a bed with rumpled covers. They give each other naughty glances while walking through New York City. What will happen to them? Will he get sick? Will she have to choose between him and a job? I feel I have seen this movie more than once before; anyone who has watched a single episode of *Tous Mes Enfants* knows this story by heart.

In the next preview, a teenage girl is in love with a strong, fit dancing man. They are in love, but her parents do not want them to be. It looks like a sweet story—love wins in the end, of course—but not very much like real life.

"Did you ever see the original *Dirty Dancing*?" Alex asks. "My mom and my sister love that movie. I guess they remade it." I shake my head. No, I haven't seen it, but I'm quite sure I know how it ends.

Now, our movie has started. I didn't know we would be seeing one of *these* movies, where a masked killer chases down teenagers one by one, and they spend an hour and a half running for their lives. I asked Mary Agnes what *Terror Lake* was about yesterday, and she giggled and said, "It's a romantic comedy." Very funny. But these movies don't scare me; they *bore* me.

Alex and I are not touching, but we are sitting very close. There's really no choice—this is an old theater, and the seats are not very large. If he makes his "move," what will I do? I don't want to create a scene and embarrass both of us. If Alex is a gentleman about it, I will let him put his arm around me, but no more.

I take a quick peek at him. He looks quite nervous, actually. Tense as a stretched rubber band, and pale, too. He doesn't seem like someone who is about to make a move; he looks like someone who wants to run away and hide.

"Do you want anything?" he whispers suddenly. "From the concession stand?" I shake my head. I'm not hungry or thirsty. Does he really want to leave the movie only ten minutes after it's begun? "I'm going to get some popcorn," he says.

"Me too!" Ira whispers. "This movie sucks."

Alex breathes a sigh of exasperation. He seems always to be irritated with Ira. Are they friends or not?

They are gone for eight or ten minutes; half of the people in the movie are already dead. But by the time Alex comes back to his seat with a bag of popcorn, a Coke for himself, and a lemonade for me—"In case you get thirsty," he says—there is a pause in the action. Ira sits, for some reason, behind us. We are one group, but are now sitting in not two, but three rows? So odd. And these people find Haitian culture strange?

Alex takes a deep breath, probably relieved that nothing too scary is happening. The camera now follows a new couple, who are driving toward the lake house where the chase happened. They are navigating a deserted road, unaware of the terrible death that awaits them there. She's a long-legged redhead, and he wears a backward baseball cap and has an ugly dot of beard hair on his chin. He tells silly jokes, and the girl laughs, but she slaps at his hands when he tries to grope and grab at her. Alex had better not be getting any ideas, because if I slap at his hands, it won't be a joke. My slaps hurt.

I look at the row in front of us. Mary Agnes is leaning so far into Nomura, she is nearly in his lap. He sits as stiff as a soldier, not pushing Mary Agnes away, not pulling her toward him, either. But Mary Agnes has never needed encouragement, has she?

In the next scene in the movie, the redhead and the baseball-cap boy are looking around the abandoned house in the middle of the woods. Everything is covered in dust and dirt, but there is a half-eaten plate of food sitting on a messy table. The girl is scared, but the boy is still joking around, bouncing on a rusty iron bed and trying to get her to "try it out" with him. The girl ignores him and fixes her eyes on an old wooden chest in the corner of the room. She approaches it and begins to open it up, while the music on the soundtrack gets louder and scarier. Because the trunk is locked, the boy begins to pry at it with some kind of bar, and finally, as he breaks the lock, a cat jumps out of the trunk, right onto the girl's face.

"Aaah!" Alex yells, holding his arms up as if the cat is going to pounce at him through the screen.

Without thinking, I reach out and grab his hand. "Are you okay?" I whisper.

At first, I can't tell who has scared Alex more: the crazy cat or me. But then he takes a deep breath, smiles, and squeezes back. "Yeah," he says. "Thanks."

21

Pretending to Yawn

So you're gonna try to make out with her, right?" Ira asks. He's rephrased the question about ten different times since he and Nomura showed up two minutes ago. I, of course, have been waiting for them in front of the Pavilion for twenty minutes (I couldn't be late, could I? Not when Bijou's schedule is so tight). And I was so amped I barely slept last night. "Maricel said you were."

"Maricel?" I ask. "How would she know? Does she have ESP?"

"She knows because it's what you're *supposed* to do," Ira says. "Otherwise, what are we all doing here?"

"You'd rather be at home with your PlayStation, I take it?" I ask.

"Than on a group date with my sister? And I'm the weird one?"

"Ira does have a point," Nomura says. "It didn't necessarily have to be a group thing. You could have asked Bijou out yourself."

I shake my head. "I already went out with her alone once, remember?" I say. "This is a group thing because of you, not me. Or Mary Agnes, anyway." I bask in the chance to play the teacherly role normally occupied by Nomura. "You don't get it, do you? Mary Agnes has basically been stalking you ever since she found out I liked Bijou. You think she cares about Bijou and me so much that she'd be willing to go out of her way to put us together like this?"

"Well, if you put it that way . . . ," Nomura says, although he's looking for a quick way to change the subject. "But why Maricel and Ira, too?"

"Elementary, my dear Nomura," I say, stroking my chin as if a wise man's beard were there instead of seven strands of peach fuzz (and to be honest, distracting myself from my jitters over the fact that the girls will be here any second). "She got Maricel and Ira to come so the pressure would be off not just for me and Bijou, but for you. She doesn't want to scare you off."

"Not bad," Nomura says.

"So, Nomura, what's *your* move going to be?" Ira asks. "Please, tell me somebody's going to man up and try *something*."

When Ira, who still looks and acts like a ten-year-old, is telling us to "man up," I know we're all in trouble.

On our way up the stairs to the tiny theater where *Terror Lake* is playing, the girls say they need to hit the bathroom, and I'm secretly grateful for one last chance to check my hair and my resolve. Nomura, who always gets it, gives me a little breathing room, but Ira won't leave me alone.

"You're such a girl," he says as I sprinkle some water on my head and sweep my bangs off my forehead. As usual, he's got that stupid video cam out. "Checking yourself out in the mirror, like Maricel."

Despite the fact that he's filming me in this incredibly private moment, I try to keep my cool. "Maybe you should try it yourself sometime," I say. "Unless you're okay with having a nasty zit right in the middle of your nose."

"Bull. Where?" he says.

Once he realizes I'm pranking him, I say, "Now will you please turn off that stupid camera? Whatever winds up happening today, I don't want it on film."

"Fine, fine," he says, turning it off.

"We don't need another Rocky and Trevor situation," Nomura says.

"Huh? What situation?" asks Ira.

Nomura and I get him up to speed on the nutty

comments about "brown sugar" and immigration marriages. I'm the one who notices that his stupid camera is still recording.

"Ira," I say. "Turn that thing off. And erase those stupid videos, please. God."

···———ꙮꙮ———···

Once we're in the theater, Ira insists on sitting next to Bijou and me. First, he grilled me about making a move on Bijou, and now he insists on getting a front-row seat to the action? I swear, I don't understand what goes on in the kid's brain sometimes. I can literally smell his breath right now (if I'm not mistaken, his lunch was peanut butter smeared on a sesame bagel), and believe me, any knowledge of Ira's gastronomic goings-on does not put me in a romantic mind-set.

The previews are okay. I try to forget that Ira is two millimeters away from me and concentrate on the fact that Bijou *is*. I try to keep the chat casual. I figure, if she and her mom have watched every episode of *All My Children*, they must have seen the all-time-favorite girlie movie *Dirty Dancing*, but no dice. Still, Bijou seems relaxed and happy enough to be hanging out, so I try to let her mellowness rub off on me, and it seems to be working.

But then *Terror Lake* starts, and I instantly regret not trying to get Mary Agnes to choose a different movie. There's no warm-up, no scenes of teenagers having fun on their way to a house out in the woods. Nope, right away, some blond girl is about to open a closet. The camera shows her from several different angles, reaching for the door handle, thinking better of it, then reaching again. What should take three seconds is drawn out into a long minute of torture. In real life, would the redhead take this long to see what is in store for her? Never. You see a closet door, you open it, you shut it; you take control. But in movies like this, which are *specifically designed to freak out people like me*, the moment stretches into infinity and beyond.

I come up with the brilliant idea of going to get popcorn and Cokes, and excuse myself to Bijou.

Ira, of course, comes bounding after me. Why? He *loves* spatter-flicks like this; he should be in nerd heaven by now. But he's got something else on his oddball brain.

"When are you gonna man up?" he asks me. The concession guy is putting about two gallons of butter on Ira's popcorn, which I guess Ira considers a manly amount.

"Seriously, Ira, why do you care? You're the least masculine guy in this entire movie theater. The only manly things you've ever done have happened in *Call of Duty*."

"Whatever. You and Nomura have girls, and I don't. But when I do, you won't see *me* acting like such a nervous wimp."

"Yeah, we'll see." I'm seething, but it's well established that I'm bad at comebacks. *Why are we even friends at all?* is what I'm wondering.

I order my popcorn, asking for the tiniest amount of butter, figuring that if Bijou is anything like Dolly, she won't touch it if there's an ocean of buttery fat dripping down the bag. As for Ira, I go for the silent treatment, also something I learned from over a decade of living with my sweet sister. We pay for our stuff and head back up to the theater in silence. Before I walk into Bijou's row, I say, "Find somewhere else to sit, man," and for once, Ira actually listens.

Thank God there's a break in the action when I find my seat again. I hand Bijou a lemonade, settle into the chair, and contemplate pretending to yawn. I think back to the source of that information. While Nomura is my best friend and a proven genius in many areas, he has even less than the tiny amount of romantic experience I do. He recommended calling Bijou at home, which turned out to be a bad move. So I rely on his wisdom for the sole reason that I have nobody else to turn to. Possibly not the best strategy in the world?

Pretending to yawn seems completely ridiculous, like a circus trick invented by dorks. A loser move performed only by lame guys (not that Nomura is lame, but perhaps his advice sometimes is) who are so afraid of rejection, they need to disguise their actual desires with shenanigans, with clumsy sleight of hand. No, Alex Schrader will not be performing any circus tricks today. No shenanigans for Alex.

And then Ira's voice pops back in my head, and I wonder if, in his words, I'm not manning up. And then I do something even less manly: scream like a four-year-old girl when this absolutely freaky-looking cat jumps out of an old wooden trunk and pounces on some poor girl's face. When the scream comes out of my mouth, I think, *I have ruined it. Again.*

But then Bijou grabs my hand, and a shock of sensation rushes through my entire body. Did she do it on purpose? She must have. Absolutely. She's trying to comfort me, and as I realize that our bare skin is touching, I start to feel less like a four-year-old girl and more like the luckiest guy on the planet.

"Are you okay?" she asks.

And I think, *Now I am.* But what I say is, "Yeah. Thanks."

Then, I up the ante and make a move of my own. I don't need to do a fake yawn; I've got everything I need right here. We're already touching, after all. I take a slow breath in, then interlace her fingers within mine. I feel her sit up in her seat—she's a little surprised, and I would have been, too—but once our hands are intertwined, she seems to be liking it well enough. I stroke my thumb along the outside of her hand, and she squeezes more tightly.

Nothing much happens after that, at least nothing easy to describe. But I learn quickly that there's a whole universe of awesomeness that lives inside that simple phrase "holding hands." We squeeze, we tickle, we caress, we stroke, and a chain reaction of tiny electric currents goes up my arm, into my shoulders and chest. Suddenly the supposedly scary movie taking place on-screen seems as distant as the moon. Ready to hide under my seat only a few minutes ago, I now want this idiotic horror film to last forever.

I can honestly say that I've never felt this close to another person, and all we're actually doing is holding hands. That's not even first base, is it? But who cares? Holding hands with someone you like? It's completely amazing.

Something crazy happens on-screen, but I barely even register it. "Are you scared?" Bijou whispers, so close it tickles my eardrum.

"No, not anymore," I say. "Are you?"

…… ℓℓℓℓ ……

We're walking along Windsor Place, girls in front, boys behind.

Ira and Nomura are comparing notes on the movie when I hear Mary Agnes say to Maricel and Bijou, "Nothing happened yet. I need to give him more *time*."

To which Bijou responds, "Please, Mary Agnes. We need to get back."

I check my phone: it's four forty. I know Bijou needs to be back at Mary Agnes's place before five thirty, but that's only a five-minute walk from here. If I were walking beside her, still holding hands (as soon as the movie was over, Mary Agnes and Maricel bum-rushed Bijou, and we were instantly back to the bleak days of gender segregation), I would tell her not to worry. I know this neighborhood almost as well as I know Ditmas, and I won't let us get too far away.

We stop in front of Uncle Louie G's, an ice-cream parlor with a giant mural of a pudgy bald man eating a scoopful from a cup. "Oooh, let's get some," Mary Agnes says. "John, buy me a cone? We can share it." It's hilarious that she calls Nomura "John," like he's forty years old or something. Nomura will never be a "John." Nomura is Nomura is Nomura.

"I'm not superhungry," Nomura says, either clueless or deliberately trying to escape Mary Agnes's sticky web. I give him a jab, though. I couldn't care less about ice cream right now, but it might give me another chance to break out of the boys-only ranks and get close to Bijou.

But Bijou says, "We should be getting back," and she looks like she means it. She's not having fun anymore. *But we still have at least a half hour!* I want to scream. *Lady Bijou, I, Sir Alex Schrader, will see to it that you are safely delivered in prompt fashion to the meeting place previously decided upon by yourself and your stern uncle!*

"Share one with me, then, please?" Mary Agnes asks Nomura, batting her lashes like a lovesick puppy.

"Okay, okay," Nomura relents.

"Mary Agnes, we really need to get back," Bijou says. "Please."

"Okay, we gotta be out of here anyway," Maricel says, maybe trying to help Bijou out. "Come on, Ira." Maricel kisses us, and Ira waves good-bye. He and Maricel cross the street to head to the subway.

Mary Agnes holds out her hand to Bijou. "Here, you can have the key. Alex can walk you home. Let yourself in the front door. I'll be back in fifteen minutes, max."

I check my phone again. It's four fifty. We'll be back at Mary Agnes's in plenty of time.

"My uncle can't come back to see me there alone. And I don't want your mom seeing me come back alone, either. She will be back in ten minutes, yes?"

I hadn't realized Mary Agnes's mom figured into the plan.

"Yeah, I guess you're right." Mary Agnes puts on a look that says, *Okay, we'll do it your way, but I don't have to like it.* "You and your strict uncle," she mutters, although she was really the only one who wanted ice cream.

The four of us take a right on Seventeenth Street and walk north toward Eighth Avenue. Bijou and I in front, Mary Agnes and Nomura following us. Once we turn the corner, we'll only be five blocks away from Mary Agnes's.

"Did you like the movie?" Bijou asks, still stressed but at least trying to keep things light.

I kick a leaf, sweeping it from the sidewalk into the gutter. "To tell you the truth, I hate movies like that," I say. "Scary movies. Could you tell?"

"Maybe a little." She laughs.

"Really?" Suddenly, I'm worried she might judge me for not being enough of a badass to sit through *Terror Lake* without freaking out.

"I was probably more frightened than you," she lies.

"I've always been freaked out by horror movies, ever since I was a little kid." It's actually a relief to tell the truth about it. I mean, really—who cares? I wouldn't even want to be with a girl who judges me for my horror-film phobia. "Ever since I was little, I just . . . didn't like them. But how about you? You didn't seem to mind."

"You can get some actors, some lights, a camera, and make a movie. Add some music, make it scary. But it is not real life. In real life, I have seen far worse. These are the things that scare me. To see a man dying of thirst. To see a little girl die of cholera because there is no clean water to be found in an entire country. *That* is a horror movie."

I don't know quite how to respond to that. I look at the sidewalk again, unsure of what to say. Finally, I just take her hand. And there it is: that same electric current, shooting up my arm, making me want to cry out with joy. "Do you want to talk about it?" I ask, suddenly guilty that I can be feeling so good when Bijou is reliving such difficult memories. "About what happened, with the earthquake?"

"Not really."

"Okay. Sorry." Bijou squeezes my hand, showing me I don't have to be.

"Maybe I will tell you someday. But for now, just know this: to see people die, it changes you. Certain things that seem small, like the look on your mother's face when she greets you in the morning, or the taste of a cup of tea, become much more important. And the things you thought you cared about, some of them do not matter at all."

"Do you miss her? Your mother?"

"Of course I do, yes. I miss her every day."

"But you can visit her, right?"

She doesn't answer right away, and I don't push it. Maybe it's crazy-expensive to fly to Haiti, and she can't afford to jump on a plane any time she feels homesick. "For now," she says, "I must make America my home."

We're still a full block away, and Bijou stops in her tracks and squints up the street. Then she drops my hand like it's on fire and puts her arm in front of me, blocking me from taking another step.

"What is it?" Mary Agnes whispers. It's obvious Bijou sees something, someone up ahead—not her uncle, I hope!

"Alex, Nomura, turn around and walk away," Bijou

says. "Mary Agnes, walk with me." We're a little slow on the uptake, standing here staring at her. "Please, let's go!"

"Bye," I say, unable to come up with a wittier one-syllable final word of my second date with Bijou Doucet. And unable, somehow, to complete the single, simple task she's set out for me: to get my butt in gear and *move*.

Taking a quick look behind her, Bijou approaches me, stands on her tiptoes, and whispers in my ear. "I was hoping I could give you a good-bye kiss today, but you see, it's impossible." And just like that, she and Mary Agnes are off, half jogging down the street toward the Bradys' house.

Nomura and I hightail it in the other direction like small-time thieves. Before we've gone a half block, a car door slams behind us. "Bijou Doucet, get over here, right now!" a voice that could belong only to Uncle Pierre calls out.

I duck behind a tree and look up the street, Nomura kneeling behind me with a freaked look on his face like he's ducking stray bullets from a drive-by. A pretty sweet seventies Crown Victoria is double-parked right in front of Mary Agnes's house. Must be Pierre's, and it's not a bad ride. He's a short guy, but trim and very neatly dressed, with a snazzy knit cap sitting on his balding head. This is a guy who spends a lot of time and attention on his car and his clothes. And he also seems to have a habit, at least when his niece is involved, of showing up to appointments forty minutes early.

It's lucky Bijou had such good eyes, because there's no way the old man could have seen Nomura and me. Is there? It's impossible to tell by looking at him; all I can tell by Pierre's body language is that he's giving her one heck of a hard time. Boy, he sure is gesticulating like a wildman.

Yikes, now Mary Agnes's mom is walking up the street, too, fresh from her spa appointment, and she looks a little mad herself. Whether at Mary Agnes or Pierre, it's hard to tell. Bijou's standing there, looking at her feet, but Pierre and Mrs. Brady really seem to be getting into it. Does she have her hands on her hips? Uh-oh. I know moms, and hands on hips can never mean anything good.

Bijou looks miserable, like she already knows that whatever grief she's getting now, it's going to be ten times worse at home. And all because of this group date. She's paying a heavy price for spending a couple of hours with her friends, for catching a lame horror flick at the Pavilion. Will she look back on today and think it was worth it?

It was definitely worth it for me. This has to go down as the best day in my short life. After all, it's the day that Bijou Doucet told me she wanted, actually desired, hoped, wished (Bijou's wish is my command) to kiss me on purpose. Not to say hello or good-bye. Not to be polite. But because she wanted to.

Yes. Yes. Yes.

Yes!

Dear Alex,

I'm so sorry about the way things ended today. This is not how I wanted to say good-bye to you. (I think I told you that already. Ha ha.)

I am writing to you in my room, where my aunt and uncle think that I am working on my social studies homework. I think it is safe, though. Tonton Pierre, he does not read English so well, and Marie Claire does not at all.

We have just finished dinner, and can you think of the one thing we spoke about the entire meal? Yes, that's right, the "sin" I committed by leaving Mary Agnes's house for a few minutes (that is the phrase we used) on a sunny spring afternoon. Pierre says that I broke a promise to him by going outside, and that a promise is "a sacred thing" (I'm translating from the Kreyol). So, a sin it is. (Don't worry, he calls many things a sin. Even playing cards, which he does at least once a week, so it's not as serious as it sounds!)

The thing so strange is that after nearly an hour of being lectured to by this man who wants to keep me inside all day like a prisoner, I began almost to feel bad for *him*. Can you imagine this?

But really, I do believe Tonton Pierre felt more bad than I did. He was angry at first, but very quickly, he became almost sad. He says he misses my mother, that he made a promise (this is his favorite word) to "his only sister" that he would protect me "as if you were my own." I tell you, Alex, he looked as if he was about to cry, even after I apologized a hundred times and told him I will never do it again.

Oh, also: Pierre swears to me that he was not trying to catch me in a lie. After dropping me off at Mary Agnes's, he had an appointment with his accountant, who has an office in Park Slope, not far away from the Bradys'. The meeting went longer than he thought it would, and he thought it would be silly for him to return to Flatbush, only to turn around a few minutes later to pick me up. So, starting at 4:45 (only five minutes before we returned!), he begin to wait outside Mary Agnes's house. He did not knock on the door, because he said he did not want to disturb my time with my girlfriends. His plan was to read his newspaper and wait until 5:30, knocking on the door only at the time we had agreed to. But when he see me with Mary Agnes (thank God he did not see you and Nomura. Can you imagine how much worse this would be?), he got out of the car and started to go crazy.

Mary Agnes's maman came home a moment later, and he go a bit crazy with her also. He said she should have known where Mary Agnes and her friends were at all times, that it is her responsibility to "protect my niece" as well as her own daughter. The woman was shocked. Speechless. Looked at my uncle like he was a lunatic. She apologized over and over, and finally, we left. I am so embarrassed, Alex.

Anyway, Marie Claire, my aunt, saved me as she does so often. She calmed my uncle down, let him see that this was not the end of the world. "Girls need their friends," she said. (Of course, she has no idea that not all of my friends are girls!) After much talk, she convinced him not to punish me. For now.

But I'm afraid that seeing each other will only become more difficult. I really like you, Alex. I want to see more of you. But we are going to have to be even more careful. I don't want to get into trouble. And I don't want to hurt Tonton Pierre, either. He is only doing what he considers his duty. I don't want to keep lying to him. It feels wrong, and bad. Even mean.

I will continue to write you, though, stopping by our Gran Bwa on my way home from school each day. And if any creative ideas come from your brilliant mind, please know that I am ready to hear them. I would like to see you again.

Soon.

Bisous (this mean "kisses" en français, but you must know this already?),

Bijou

22

Brainstorming Masterpieces

Don't worry," Mary Agnes says. "There's always Musicale."

She, Maricel, and I are sitting along the back wall of the cafeteria, enjoying the sun coming through the large windows and eating meatballs in a gooey white sauce. Many West Indians, especially Jamaicans, are vegetarians. Another few months of St. Catherine's lunches, and I might have to join them.

"Tell me, what is Musicale, again?" I ask. In the last week, everyone seems to be talking about it, like it's the answer to peace and global happiness. But no one ever takes the time to explain what it actually is.

"It's a chance to show your talent to the whole school," Mary Agnes says. "To both schools."

"Is it, how do you say . . . mandatory?" I ask.

Mary Agnes and Maricel exchange looks. "Well, not technically," Mary Agnes says. "But who wouldn't want to? It's our only cool tradition."

"Basically, it's an excuse for boys and girls to make out in the catacombs," Maricel says.

"That, too," Mary Agnes says, giggling. "Well, that, primarily. Especially now, since your grumpy uncle has made your love life so difficult."

"Love life?" I say. "I don't want a love life." I wish she would not make fun of Tonton Pierre. If I am going to have to deceive him, I certainly don't want to talk about it in front of the whole world. And Mary Agnes is not always so generous as she seems. She's looking for ways to be with the boy she likes, too, but she is too afraid to ask *him* on a "solo date."

"Anyway, back to the topic," Maricel says. "It's pretty much free-form. You pick your group—groups are encouraged, because there are only ten soloists allowed, and those are usually musical-prodigy types who spend all their non-school time practicing piano or whatever—write up a one-paragraph summary of what you're going to do, then submit it to the Musicale Committee."

"That's Mr. Sinclair, from St. Chris's," Mary Agnes says. "And Ms. Alonzo, our music teacher."

"They have a thing for each other," Maricel says.

"They totally do, and get this: they're the Musicale

practice monitors," Mary Agnes says. "Which means we spend more time flirting in the catacombs than we do brainstorming masterpieces."

"What are the catacombs?" I ask.

"This building is superold, and there's a network of, like, underground tunnels that somebody dug here a long time ago," Maricel says.

"That sounds . . . scary," I say.

"It's not," Mary Agnes says. "In the olden days, monks prayed down there or something. But the school fixed them up a few years ago, and now it's like a nice, finished basement. Lots of practice rooms for . . . brainstorming."

"For example, flirting and/or making out with cute boys," Maricel says.

"Yep," Mary Agnes says. "Lots of narrow hallways, and twists and turns to get lost in. And nice, hygienic spots to pursue both musical and nonmusical interests."

"You two are both terrible!" I say.

"Okay, now that *that's* been established," Mary Agnes says, "what are we going to do?"

"I say we go for something cross-cultural," Maricel says. "Like a mash-up. I can work on my DJ skills."

"Absolutely," Mary Agnes says. "Sinclair and Alonzo will love that. They're having a cross-cultural romance of their own, after all. And what are we, if not diverse? We've got a white girl, a Haitian, a couple Dominicans, and the cutest Japanese boy in Brooklyn." She winks. So silly. "Bijou, didn't you say Alex is pretty good on that Haitian drum thingy?"

"Yes, he's not bad." I can't help but smile. He was so cute, drumming with his eyes closed, like my brother and his friends.

"And you can dance, right?" Mary Agnes's eyes open wide. Her excitement always scares me a little bit. She could have played a role in *Terror Lake*.

I frown, imagining myself performing Haitian traditional dance for several hundred Episcopal middle school students and their families.

.... ℓℓℓℓℓ ....

Ms. Barrington, my English teacher, lets our seventh-period study hall out early, so I get to leave school at two forty-five. This is good. I can use the extra time to stop by the Gran Bwa to drop off my letter to Alex (and see if he's left anything there for me!), and still be home early. Pierre won't be home until after six, but Marie Claire will, and she will be expected to give her husband the most detailed of reports on my comings and goings, especially since last Saturday.

What a lucky thing to have some extra time! I have promised Marie Claire I would pick up her dry cleaning on Flatbush before meeting Jou Jou at Guillaume's. I decide to walk by St. Christopher's to see if, by chance, Alex and I might go together. He doesn't even know I will stop by our Gran Bwa, or that I'm going to sit in on his lesson.

Alex is not here, but I do spot another couple of boys lingering on the front steps. I try not to make eye contact with them, but it's too late; they've already looked up. No, no, no. It's Rocky and Trevor.

"Hey, Bijou," says Rocky.

Then Trevor stands up. "I'll catch you tomorrow, Rock," he says.

"You sure you know what you're doing, man?" the spiky one asks.

"Watch and learn." Do they think I cannot hear them? Or do they simply not care?

"Hey, wait up a second," the tall one calls out to me. Do I just keep on walking? Ignore him completely?

"It's Bijou, right?" he asks. I force him to walk alongside me; I do not make extra room for him on the sidewalk. "You remember me, from the dance? I'm Trevor."

"I remember," I say. "So?" My attitude toward him is not cold. It is subfreezing.

"Oh, I get it, totally," he says. "That was a completely uncool situation. But I wasn't really the one giving Schrader a hard time. That was Rocky, remember?" He puts on a sad face. "I guess I need to start picking better friends."

"You don't need to start with me. There are lots of other people you can make friends with." The subway is only two blocks away, on Clark Street. I have no idea where this

Trevor lives, but I pray he leaves me at the station. If I have to sit with him on the train, I'll go crazy. Why did Ms. Barrington have to let us out early again?

"Listen, we got off to a wrong start, and I'm sorry about that," the boy says, brushing back his hair behind his ear. He knows he is handsome, which makes him almost ugly. To me, anyway. "But I'm not the guy you think I am. I'm actually pretty nice."

"Are you nice to Jenna?" I ask. "She's your girlfriend, right?"

"I never know with her." Again, the sad face. "Sometimes she is, sometimes she isn't."

"Well, I'm not looking for any new friends." At last, the Clark Street station is only another half block. "And I'm in a hurry to get home, so—"

Then, out of nowhere, Trevor grabs my hand. "Stay and talk for a second," he says.

"What are you doing?" I say, yanking my hand away.

"Hey, sorry, I didn't mean it like that." He smiles. "I . . . really like you."

"Well, thank you, but it's not polite to reach for a girl's hand, unless it's offered to you first." Finally, the elevator. Unless this rich-looking white boy plans on following me to "scary" Flatbush, I only just have time to reach our Gran Bwa and still get to Monsieur Guillaume's.

"Is this what you did with Alex?" he asks. "Play hard to get?"

I don't respond, but I'm sure he can see the look of disgust on my face.

Suddenly, Jenna appears beside him. "Hey," she says, shoving him while giving me a dirty look. "Where have you been? I've been looking for you."

"Well, you found me." Trevor smiles, taking her hand.

I turn away and step into the elevator. I cannot escape from these two soon enough.

"What were you doing, talking to her?" I hear Jenna say behind me.

"I wasn't 'talking to her.' I just ran into her on my way to the newsstand in the station. They're the only place that carries sour-cream-and-onion Utz."

I'm looking down into the station, so I don't see or hear Jenna's reaction. The elevator takes me down, down, down, away from this boy, away from his foolish games. I shake my head, thinking about Jenna. Now she will hate me even more, and for nothing.

Please God, tell me that, deep inside, not all boys are like this. Because I am on my way to see a boy right now who is quite different.

23

Lessons

As I'm leaving school, I run into Rocky and Angela. They're lounging out on St. Chris's front steps, where they always hang out, draped over each other, lazily smacking gum.

"Hey, here comes the big man," Rocky says, leaning back against the steps. He toys with Angela's hair. She swats at his hand, like the girl from *Terror Lake*. "How's that little girlfriend of yours?"

"Bijou?" Darn, I shouldn't have said her name. Now I've put a target on Bijou's back. And mine, too.

"She's adorable," Rocky says in that voice where you can't tell whether he's being serious or not. Angela flashes him a look. "I mean, she's not a goddess, like you, but she's . . . interesting."

"She's a snob," Angela said.

"Who's a snob?" asks Trevor. He and Jenna plop down on the steps.

"Bijou, the new girl," Angela says. Then, nodding toward Trevor, "So where was *he* hiding?"

"He was at the subway station, buying chips." Jenna eyes Trevor suspiciously. "Or so he says."

Trevor holds up a bag of Utz and puts on a "Who? Me?" expression.

"And yeah, she is a snob," Jenna says. "We just saw her. She refused to even look at me."

"Just because she doesn't like *you*," Rocky snarks, "doesn't make her a snob." I have to agree with him there.

"She is definitely stuck-up," Jenna says. Are we even talking about the same person here? Bijou's not stuck-up; she's shy. "I was so nice to her the first week she was here, and now she thinks she's all that."

"Oh my God, I'm so tired of hearing you guys complain about her," Trevor says. "You're just mad because (a) she didn't join your little clique at the drop of a hat—"

"Not cool, Trevor," Angela says, while Jenna looks at her boyfriend in total shock.

"—and (b) now the two of you have competition for who is the hottest girl in your class. There, I finally said it."

Jenna puts her hand up to her mouth. For a second it looks like she's about to gag. "You are . . . such . . . a . . . complete jerk!" she says, before picking up her backpack and running away. She looks genuinely hurt. I know it's Jenna Minaya, but I actually feel sorry for her. For anyone dumb enough to pick Trevor Zelo as a boyfriend.

"Wow, dude, way to overshare," Rocky says, shaking his head.

"What are you thinking?" Angela asks. "You should run after her right now and apologize."

"Eh, maybe later," Trevor says. "She's really been annoying lately. And admit it, Angela. It's true: she's just jealous."

"Whatever," Angela says, picking up her things.

"Now you're going, too?" Rocky asks. "What'd *I* do?"

"Nothing," Angela says, walking off. "You two deserve each other."

Rocky and I stare at each other for a moment, probably both wondering how exactly we wound up alone together.

"See, Schrader?" Rocky says, smirking. "Even when you're popular, girls can still be a total pain. If you ever manage to get a girlfriend, you'll see."

"No way," I say. "I'm not like you guys."

"Yeah, you are. You're exactly like us."

-----ᵒᵉᵉᵉᵉ-----

By the time I arrive at Monsieur Guillaume's, I'm thoroughly winded. It's a long trip from the Parkside stop when you're not riding in a dollar van. I pause outside Guillaume's to catch my breath, take a quick look at my reflection in the shop window—if Bijou's there already, I need to be looking my best—and check my watch.

Yikes, it's already almost three thirty, and I told my mom I'd be home by five. She thinks I'm studying math with

Nomura, of course, not studying rara music in a discount clothing store on the "bad side" of Flatbush Avenue and hoping for a glimpse of my hopefully-soon-to-be girlfriend.

I wave hello to Monsieur Guillaume, who's whacking away at the old cash register like it's willfully disobeying him. Bijou's not here, not yet, anyway, but I don't ask Jou Jou about her. He's taking time out of his day to teach me, and he's only charging me a measly ten bucks (all I can afford without asking Mom for cash). I want to let him know that I am here for my lesson, not just for Bijou, even though it's hard to concentrate, knowing she might walk in the door any second.

"You doing real good, Alex," Jou Jou says. We're not down in the basement, but up in the store, sharing Jou Jou's rada. He's on one side of the drum, I'm on the other.

"Yes, he is," says Guillaume. "Alex, you sure don't *look* Haitian. What'm I missing here, son?"

Jou Jou and I laugh along with him, but only for a second. Jou Jou's kind of intense when he's teaching. He might seem like a lighthearted dude, but when it comes to rara music, he's all business.

He shows me a beat he calls raboday. "No, Alex, don't cup your hand, see?" He pulls the drum closer to him and demonstrates. "Like this, see? Elbows in a little . . . and pull your left thumb in. Otherwise, you gonna whack it when it's time for you to use the stick."

I'm going to learn how to use a drumstick, too? It's exciting to think about being good at this one day, but it's also hard to imagine. He and Bijou grew up with this music, after all, while to me it's completely foreign. I'm not going to become awesome at it overnight, just like I'm not going to wake up tomorrow and speak to Nomura in fluent Japanese. Still, though, I *want* to learn, definitely a first for Alex Schrader.

I practice the raboday pattern for a couple of minutes, and somewhere deep down, buried under the muck of my sloppy mistakes, I recognize something resembling actual rhythm. My whole body vibrates as I slap the cow-skin head and feel it snap against the rada's wooden rim.

"That's it, that's it," Jou Jou says. "Now you need to work on that about thirty more hours."

I give him a look of shock. What would the females in my house do if I started a thirty-hour-a-week drumming regimen? Jou Jou laughs.

"When am I going to study?" I ask, not knowing whether he's fully serious or not. "You know, for school?"

"School?" Jou Jou asks. Then he nods toward the drum. "*This* is school."

I hear the door swing open. Bijou walks in the room, wearing her school uniform and carrying not only a ridiculously heavy-looking backpack, but also an armful of dry cleaning.

"Need help with that?" I ask.

"No, I'm okay." She smiles, but she looks a little stressed. "I don't want to interrupt, but Jou Jou, can you please call Marie Claire? She expects me any minute, and I want to let her know I am with you."

"Yes, sister, no worries." He gets up and kisses her hello, then starts dialing.

"Don't tell her who your student is!" she whispers. Jou Jou looks at her like she's told him the most obvious thing in the world.

While Jou Jou is on the phone, I get *my* hello kisses. Nice! I'm getting to be a pro at this.

"Everything okay?" I ask.

"Yes, yes. I got your note and came right over. Everything is fine, as long as they think I'm with Jou Jou, and only Jou Jou."

"Your uncle was pretty mad about the movie, huh?"

"Movie? He has no idea about that." She laughs. "If he knew we left the house for two full hours, he would have had a heart attack."

"Is it really that bad?"

"Tonton Pierre? You know, this is the first time I am living with him. He means well. He gets angry quickly, but he forgets quickly, too. He doesn't *want* to be mad; he is only doing what he thinks my maman would want." She nods toward Jou Jou. "And as long as I'm with family, it's fine."

Jou Jou hangs up. "All good," he says. "Auntie say be home in a half hour, though."

"Okay," Bijou says. "Can you give me a ride?"

"Sorry, Bijou, I can't. We have rehearsal here at six, and I've got to pick up some flyers at the copy shop first." Then, a trace of a smile. "Alex, you can be a gentleman and walk my sister home, can't you?"

"Uh, yeah." I can definitely be a gentleman. Anything for ten minutes of unsupervised time with Bijou. "No problem."

"Oh, and Alex, I was thinking of something. No promises, okay? But if you keep up with your practicing, maybe I can ask Fabian and see if you could join us for the first rara this year. May thirtieth, in Prospect Park. Would you like that?"

"I would love that," I say. Wow.

————— ℓℓℓℓℓ —————

But not as much as I love walking Bijou home, even though I'm about to keel over from carrying both her backpack and mine.

"You sure you are okay?" Bijou asks.

"Yeah, yeah, fine." The truth is, it feels like I'm carrying a small refrigerator, but I can't tell Bijou that. Honesty isn't always the best policy when you're trying to be at your most gentlemanly.

Bijou laughs. "Well, you don't have to do it, but in one way, you are lucky."

"Yeah?" I ask. "How so?"

"We are here."

"Oh really?" I'm torn between immense relief that I can put down her so-heavy-there-must-be-a-dead-body-in-it backpack and regret that our time together is almost up. "Is this your house?" I nod toward a brown-shingled three-family.

Bijou gives me a *get serious* look. "I can't take you right in front of my house. My aunt would see me, or a neighbor would recognize me." She nods down the street. "See over there? *That's* my building." A brightly painted white Victorian. Nice place. Bigger than ours. "Uh-oh, that's Marie Claire. Come on." Sure enough, a fifty-something black lady walks out the front door with a trash bag in hand.

Bijou takes me by the wrist, and we duck into the doorway of the three-family. "We wait here a moment, then I go," she whispers, the tiny wind of her breath tickling my cheek. We're even closer now than we were in the movie theater. I don't want her to get in trouble, but can we stay here forever, huddled in this Flatbush foyer?

"Alex, write me tomorrow," she says. Marie Claire has gone back in the house, so it's safe. No more huddling.

"Okay, sure. Yeah."

She's so close to me that I can't help it. I put my arms

around Bijou's waist. It feels right. I'm looking directly at her, and she's looking back. I've never seen her eyes this close before, never touched any part of her body except her arm hairs and her hand. But now we're joined as one, our hands meeting on her hips, our fingers interlocked.

Then, just like that, she moves two inches closer and kisses me. On the mouth. Her lips are soft, and they linger on mine for a moment, before she steps back and breaks the seal of our kiss.

And she is gone. And I cannot move. And I cannot stand. I stay here, long enough to watch her run off without looking back, open her front door, and disappear. And still, I cannot move. That was no peck. It was a real kiss. My first real kiss.

I look at my watch. It's five thirty. I'm late! Mom's not going to be happy, but who cares? I am totally immobile. I don't think my legs even work anymore.

I have kissed a girl.
I have kissed Bijou.
Bijou has kissed me.
My first kiss.
Our first kiss.

 24

When You're Busted, You're Busted

I head up the front steps, put my key in the front door, and start to push, when the door opens all by itself. It's Mom, waiting there for me, with an expression on her face that is beyond unhappy. She looks more like a mobster than a mom.

"I told you not to lie to me again, Alex," she says.

I don't say a thing. I walk past her as quietly as I can.

Seriously? I have to add my own mother to the list of people determined to give me a hard time about anything and everything having to do with Bijou and me? Do parents think it's their personal mission to prevent their kids from growing up into responsible adults with actual lives?

"Alex, answer me. What do you have to say for yourself?"

I think as clearly as I can, considering that I *just had my first kiss*. "I told you I was going to a movie with Ira and Nomura, and I *was* going to a movie with Ira and Nomura."

"Wait, you're talking about last Saturday?" She looks

like she's about to order a hit on me, gangster-style. "I wasn't even talking about the movie, Alex." Oops. "Was there anyone there besides you and your guy friends?"

All right, when you're busted, you're busted. "Bijou, Mary Agnes, and Maricel."

"What?!?"

"I didn't lie. I just didn't tell you every single person who wound up coming."

"Oh please, Alex. Like Bijou wasn't the entire reason you were there. It was a *horror* movie. You were terrified of Harry Potter, for God's sake."

"Thanks for pointing that out, Mom."

"Were you with her again this afternoon?" she asks. "Because I know you weren't with Nomura. I called over there, and his mom told me she hadn't seen you in two weeks."

"Yeah, I was." I tell her about everything: the drum lesson, the walk home.

Correction: I tell her about everything except the very best part. I'm allowed to keep some things to myself.

"Alex, I don't know what's gotten into you since you met that girl, but you're turning into a habitual liar."

"I didn't lie. I just didn't tell the whole truth."

"Alex, omitting the truth *is* a lie." She takes a deep breath, gathers herself. "You are forbidden to see her, or her brother, until I say otherwise. And for the next three weeks, you're not to see *anybody* outside of school. Not

Nomura, not Ira, not anybody. You'll come straight home after classes each day, you'll do your homework, you'll go to bed."

"Is that all?" From past experience, I know challenging her, or using sarcasm at all, is a big mistake. So why am I doing it?

"Actually, it's not." She takes two steps toward me and holds out her hand. "I'll have your cell phone, please."

"What? For how long?"

"For as long as you're grounded."

"What? Three weeks without a phone?" Who ever would have thought that my mom would be as bad as Uncle Pierre? Correction: worse than Pierre. "You're doing all this because I like a girl?"

"No. Because you've lied to me repeatedly." Her words splatter me like paintball pellets. "Because your interest in this girl has made you lose sight of what's right and what's wrong. End of story."

End of story? Not quite. I might have to suspend drum lessons for a while, but there's still our Gran Bwa. And Musicale rehearsals, which take place during school hours. I've still got two weeks before the actual performance, where Mom and Dolly will, of course, be in the audience.

After forbidding me to see Bijou, it'll be quite a shock to see me sharing a stage with her. But I'll cross that bridge when I come to it.

Alex,

Oh, that was a close call, wasn't it?

When I walked in, Marie Claire said it was a miracle I could carry my backpack and all those clothes from the dry cleaner's to Guillaume's and back. She felt my arm muscle and said, "You been working out, niece?" Funny, right?

I'm glad you come from a family that doesn't watch you so closely.

I can't wait to see you for our first Musical (is that how you spell it?) rehearsal. You're bringing your drum, right? Now it's your turn to carry around something heavy all the day long.

I miss you. Tuesday is too far away. Leave me a note.

Bijou

P.S. You are the first boy I ever kissed. I liked it. I'm glad it was you, Alex.

25

Honing Our Act

Jeez, everybody's got a talent except me," Mary Agnes says. We are in the catacombs. I was expecting a scary dungeon from the girls' description, like something from *Terror Lake*. But it is only a basement with narrow hallways and low ceilings. Mary Agnes exaggerates *everything*. "Alex plays the drum thingy, Bijou's a terrific dancer, and Maricel has her DJ thing." She smiles at Nomura like a proud mother. "John is an all-around genius and a pretty decent rapper, if I do say so myself. And Ira can do video projections. But what do I do?"

"You're the one who brought us all together," Nomura says.

"And you're the one who bosses us around," Alex says, laughing.

"You make sure we get here on time," Maricel says.

". . . and bring all the stuff we're supposed to," says Ira.

"Yeah, but onstage, nobody sees that," Mary Agnes says. "So it doesn't really count."

"What is the word in English?" I ask. "Choreographer?" Mary Agnes shrugs.

"How about executive producer?" Nomura asks.

"Ooh, I like that," says Mary Agnes. "That'll do. That'll do quite nicely."

I resist asking, *Executive producer of . . . what, exactly?* Because we have been doing a lot of talking so far, but not much of what I would call rehearsing. Alex played one of the beats that Jou Jou has been teaching him, and I began to move—only Mary Agnes would call it dancing—along to the rhythm. Maricel began to sing a sweet, lazy melody in Spanish, and Ira told us he could make a little movie to go along with our song for the final performance. So far, I have not heard any of Nomura's rapping, so he must have treated Mary Agnes to a private performance!

In fact, he might be treating her to it again right now, because she just pulled him out of the room and into the catacombs. "I want to show you, John. Come on." And he did. Maybe if I had grown up in this school, if I knew all its twists and turns like Mary Agnes knows the catacombs, I would pull Alex away for a moment of privacy, too. It would be nice to have time alone with him. But it doesn't feel right to go sneaking off. It doesn't even feel right to hold hands in front of the group. I try to trade glances with him when I can, but that is as far as I dare go. What I have with him is too private to share with others, whether they are friends or not.

Alex, Maricel, Ira, and I are packing up our things now. No sign of Mary Agnes and Nomura.

"Bijou, want to walk me back to St. Chris's?" Alex asks.

Ah, nice idea. At least one of us is being creative. "Yes," I say. "I'd like that."

"Okay, see you guys," Maricel says as we walk up the stairs to the main level. We wave good-bye.

When Ira, Alex, and I walk through the front doors, Ira tells him, "Dude, I've gotta talk to you. It's important."

"Can't it wait?" Alex asks.

"No, not really. I need to tell you something *now*."

Alex puts his arm around Ira's shoulder and whispers, "It needs to wait. Give us some space here. Walk back on Orange instead of Cranberry." Ira doesn't look insulted; he looks worried. He doesn't move until Alex says, "Bijou and I want to be alone for a few minutes, get it?" Ira walks off, helpless.

Once we are a block away and can see that no one else is around, we are holding hands. We laugh about the "rehearsal" and wonder whether or not we will all be making fools of ourselves.

"I don't want to give Haitian drumming a bad name," Alex says.

"Don't worry," I tease. "What you are doing, I wouldn't call 'Haitian drumming.' Not yet."

"Thanks a lot!" Alex says, tickling me. "How many years 'til I become a master drummer, you think?"

"How many *years*?" I ask. "Or how many lifetimes?"

He makes a pretend-hurt face and puts his arm around my waist, and I let my head fall on his shoulder. Even though he is only a little bit taller than me, it works.

But our schools are too close together. I can already see St. Christopher's, only a block away. Is there time for a quick kiss before we get too close? I stop and look at Alex and those beautiful blue-green eyes. I sigh and hug him. Today, a hug is enough. I breathe him in and then, though I don't want to, let him go.

"I'll be thinking of you," I say.

"Me too," he says. "All day."

We each walk backward for a few steps, not wanting to stop looking at each other. But soon enough, he is gone.

......———ℓℓℓℓℓ———...

In front of school, I see Trevor again, this time with a knowing look in his eye. As if he is waiting for me.

"How was rehearsal?" he asks, not exactly blocking my way on the steps, but not letting me pass him, either.

"I hear Alex is a real good drummer," he says, playing air drums. As if with drumsticks, not like a Haitian drummer at all.

"Yes, he is," I say. "Can you move, please? I have class."

"He isn't who you think he is," Trevor says. "Alex, I mean."

"If that's what you think, then you don't know him."

"I know Schrader pretty well. We've been in the same class since kindergarten," he says. "You've been here, what, a couple months?"

When I don't say anything, he says, "Anyway, you'll see what I mean soon enough." He slides down the banister, his feet smacking the sidewalk when he reaches the bottom. "And when you do, feel free to get in touch. Like I said, I think you're really—"

Instead of letting him finish the sentence, I run up the steps and put all my body's weight against the door, not thinking for a moment that someone might be on the other side of it.

"You idiot, watch where you're going!" Jenna yells. I hit her with the door, and the drink she was holding must have exploded because her pink T-shirt is covered in soda. "God, what do you think you're doing?"

"Oh no, Jenna, I didn't mean it," I say, not asking her what she thought *she* was doing, standing directly in front of the door like that. "It was a mistake. There was glare on the glass. I'm so sorry."

"Not as sorry as you're going to be if you don't stop flirting with my boyfriend."

Oh, so this is what she's upset about. If she only knew how wrong she was. "Jenna, I was not flirting with him. And if it were my choice, I would not even be talking to him. If you don't want us to have a conversation, tell *him* to stop talking to *me*."

"You're lying," she says. "Why would Trevor talk to *you*?" As if I am garbage. Who raised this girl?

"Since you were watching," I ask, "did it look like I came up to him? He wouldn't even let me walk by him."

"I know the truth about you, you know. I know everything."

"What are you talking about?"

"And I'm going to tell every single person, in both schools. Everyone'll finally see what a little faker you are. Let's see how popular you are after that."

I don't need to hear any more. I leave the obviously crazy girl there, her mouth wide open, syrupy soda still dripping off her skin, her clothing, even her face, as her voice echoes through the halls.

"You're going to be sorry! When I'm done, you're going to wish you never came to this school!"

Boys on Film

The next morning, Ira is waiting for me in front of school. Superstressed. Like pre-heart-attack stressed. I'd completely forgotten about this supposedly important thing he needs to tell me.

"Why haven't you been answering your cell, man?" he asks. The poor kid looks like he's about to blow a gasket.

"I didn't tell you? I'm grounded. Like, no-cell-phone-for-a-month grounded. I've been sent back to caveman times." The truth is, I've kind of liked being off the grid. Bijou and I send notes to each other from the Gran Bwa, the secret exchange place that nobody but us knows about. Going down Flatbush Avenue adds, what, another seven minutes to my route to and from school, which is no big deal. And who else do I really want to hear from, anyway? Definitely not Anxious Ira.

"I've been trying to talk to you," Ira says. "It's important."

"Listen, I do want to talk. I want to hear what you have to say, but can it wait? I've got three minutes to get to Price's class. I've been late twice already this week, and he's gonna freak on me if I'm late again."

"It can't wait!" Ira says, but I'm already halfway down the hall, toward my locker. I've got to dump off my backpack, and I should make it to my good buddy Mr. Price on time.

"It's gonna have to!" I yell over my shoulder. "Meet me at lunch!"

Why does everybody feel the sudden need to talk to me this morning? I've got maybe ninety seconds to make it to class, and Rocky and Trevor are standing right in front of my locker.

"Hello and howdy, dudes," I say, not really caring about the consequences of sassing off to these clowns anymore (Bijou gives me confidence, see?). "Would you kindly move out of the way for a second, so I can, you know, get into *my locker*?"

"Wow, Schrader, that was an all-time performance," Trevor says, moving a crucial six inches so I can open my combination lock. Needless to say, I have no idea what the heck he's talking about.

"Seriously," Rocky chimes in. "Oscar-worthy. Only thing

is, didn't you steal that line from us? That's illegal, that's, what do you call it—"

"Plagiarism," Trevor says. "Straight-up theft."

"What are you talking about?" I ask.

"You'll see soon enough," Trevor says. "But make sure our names don't get mentioned. If this comes back to us, you *will* regret it, believe me."

"Dude," Rocky says, patting Trevor on the back. "Stop stressing. He's the one who said it, and he said it *on video*. Forget the plagiarism thing. Schrader here will get sole writing credit. And he deserves it. After all, it's a friggin' masterpiece."

They cackle their way down the hall, not bothering to explain. What video? What "masterpiece"? What is going on?!

I see a bit of white sticking out of my locker vent, and right away I know it's another note. My blood freezes as I brace for what's inside. It's got to be Rocky and Trevor, right? There's got to be some connection between this supposed "performance" and the note, but what is it? I tear open the envelope and find this:

> Now everybody knows how you really feel about that stupid girl. And believe me, she is stupid. Wait till you see what happens next.
> Enjoy your day!

I head straight for English, knowing I'll see Nomura there. I can only hope that he's got a clue what Rocky and Trevor were talking about and how it relates to this note. What could the writer mean by how I "really feel"? Unlike Rocky and Trevor, I'm not into bragging about girls, and I don't think I've ever copied any of their stupid sayings— seriously, plagiarize *them*? Publicly? That'd be social suicide.

As I make my way down the hall, it seems like everyone is looking at me. Seventh and eighth graders, fifth and sixth graders, even lower schoolers, all glance in my direction. But just as quickly, their eyes dart away, like I'm an exotic but disgusting animal at whom they can't resist taking a guilty peek.

"Finally, you're here," I whisper to Nomura as he takes the seat to my left. "What is happening?"

"You . . . don't want to know," he says.

"Umm, yes, I do. Like, right now." Nomura whips out his phone and goes to YouTube. "Oh no," I say. "Is it bad?"

"It's worse than bad."

But before the video starts playing, Mr. Price stands up and clears his throat. "Mr. Nomura, kindly put the phone away. You and Mr. Schrader can watch all the videos you like after class, but this is my time."

27

Enjoy Your Dessert

I'm so sorry, sweetie," says Mary Agnes, who pulled me aside to show me the video as soon as I arrived at school this morning. "This is awful."

But for the first ten seconds, the light in the YouTube video is so low, I cannot even tell what I am looking at. A flickering light. Dark shadows. Loud, scary music that stops and starts. Spoken words in the background, too muffled to hear. The video is fifty-three seconds long. It was uploaded yesterday and has been viewed a hundred and eighty-four times. The most recent comment is, "What a creep! Who knew?"

Starting at fifteen seconds, a boy's voice begins: "She'll pretend she likes an American guy so she can stay in the country." Then a picture of me appears! "Next thing you know, she'll try to get you to marry her, so she can become a citizen. . . . stupid, right?"

"It sounds a little like . . . ," I say.

Mary Agnes puts her arm around my shoulder. I shake it off. "It doesn't sound like him, Bijou. It *is* him."

"No," I say. "I don't believe it."

I look at the user name of the person who posted the video: "RizeAgainToo." The video returns to the shadowy room, but now I can see the images a little bit better. It's a close-up of Alex and me, holding hands in the movie theater. And now the whole world can see it.

Suddenly, the scene switches to a different room, brightly lit. A close-up of Alex, speaking. The voice is definitely the same as it was from the beginning of the video. These words actually came out of his mouth.

But now he's saying, "Everybody needs a little taste of brown sugar." A box of brown sugar appears on the video, and the sound is edited so that "brown sugar" repeats and repeats, until Alex sounds like a robot. How could he have said these things? How could he do this to me?

After at least ten repetitions, the video goes back to the movie theater, showing the exact moment when Alex reached for my hand. It's still very dim, but anyone who looks hard can see everything: the way we interlaced our fingers together, the way his thumb delicately stroked the back of my hand.

Then, Alex's voice comes in again, this time with a new, shorter sentence: "Enjoy your dessert." And this one, too, repeats many times before a new, edited combination of all three sentences begins: "She'll try to get you to marry her . . . brown sugar . . . enjoy your dessert." The phrases begin to get louder and blur into each other, and the video shows our intertwined hands in the dark theater. Then Alex's brightly lit face, which changes into mine so quickly that I feel dizzy watching. The volume is louder now, booming and filled with echo. "Marry her . . . brown sugar . . . enjoy your dessert."

That must have been the longest fifty-three seconds of my life. And by the time I've watched it a second time, the number of views has gone up to two hundred and nineteen. I look around me. How many people are watching it right at this moment?

Mary Agnes is talking to me, but I can't even hear what she is saying. I want to scream, but I cannot even speak. Soon the video will have traveled beyond St. Catherine's and St. Christopher's, to my brother. To Pierre and Marie Claire.

Anyone who owns a phone can see how this boy has tricked me and made me look like a fool. How he took my feelings and threw them away like garbage.

Maman, can you see it, too? Can you see what they have done to me?

Dear Bijou,

I'm sure you've seen this ridiculous video by now. I'm so, so sorry for saying what I did, but you've got to understand, it wasn't what it looked like.

I would never say anything to hurt you.

Please write me back. I can explain everything!

Alex

28

Gentlemen

I told you Schrader wasn't who you thought he was," Trevor says, waiting for me again halfway between St. Catherine's and the Clark Street station. "Not all guys are like him, though, Bijou. Some of us are actually gentlemen."

I ignore him and keep walking. I want nothing to do with Alex, with Trevor, with any of them.

Please, please, please leave me alone.

Please, please, please don't let my aunt and uncle see the video.

Just let me be invisible.

—————— ♪♪♪♪♪ ——————

I go to that tree that Alex and I used to call our Gran Bwa. What a stupid joke that was. There is no spirit in that tree. It is an old, broken-looking thing, covered with scars and holes and ugly blemishes.

I read his note, crumple it up, and throw it in the gutter in front of Trini-Daddy's. He says he can explain everything. He says he is sorry, but an apology won't make a difference in my life. Can Alex snap his fingers and make everyone in school see me the way they saw me only forty-eight hours ago? No, he can't.

I thought I could be friends with an American boy. I thought I could trust him even though we come from such different places and have such different experiences.

I was wrong.

Bijou,

Maybe I shouldn't write again, but since I haven't heard from you in a couple days, I had to try again. I know that when you understand what happened, and how it happened, you'll see that while I might have been stupid, I wasn't trying to be mean. That's the last thing I would ever do.

I was talking to Ira and Nomura in the bathroom before the movie. And I was quoting Rocky and Trevor, repeating some terrible things that they had said about you to me earlier that week. Maybe that was my mistake, right there. I shouldn't have repeated words that ugly. I should have kept them private, where they belong.

But they were not my words; they were Rocky and Trevor's. If you think I could have said those awful things, then you never knew me in the first place.

When I saw that Ira had his camera on, I asked (demanded, actually) that he erase everything he had filmed. But he didn't. I thought I could trust him, but obviously I was wrong. He's no friend of mine. Not anymore.

But, Bijou, you've got to believe me: I'm the same person I've been all along. I'm the guy who wants to get to know you better, and the guy who knows that you have no interest whatsoever in marrying me so you can stay in the U.S.! (Sorry, a lame attempt at a joke.)

Please, please think this over. Please trust me. And write me back, okay?

Your friend, always,

Alex

 **29**

Long-Time Friends

It's Thursday, five minutes before first period. I still haven't heard a word from Bijou, and Nomura is trying to convince me that that's not entirely Ira's fault. Which is obviously insane.

"We've been friends for a long time," Nomura says. "And ever since you met Bijou, you've been a real jerk to him."

"I'm the jerk?" I ask. "He's the one who shot that stupid video. And posted it." *And ruined my life,* I almost add. "He's also the one who hasn't been showing up to school. If that doesn't scream 'guilty,' what does?"

"Let me put it this way. For the past few weeks, you've been treating Ira the way Rocky and Trevor treat the rest of us."

"Come on, you're exaggerating. It hasn't been that bad."

"Remember 'Friendship can walk the plank, matey'?" Nomura asks.

"Hold on," I say. "That was a joke."

"You have to admit, though, you've been treating Ira differently since Bijou showed up."

"Only because he has lost his mind," I say. "The video proves it. And so do these." I pull out the three anonymous notes.

Nomura pushes his glasses up against his nose. His pupils bounce back and forth like tennis balls, scanning the text. "Oh boy," he says.

"It has to be Ira, right?"

"Um, not necessarily. What makes you say that?"

"The only other logical possibility is Trevor and Rocky. I thought it was them at first. But they didn't post the video; Ira did. Plus, have you ever known them to do *anything* anonymous? They're not exactly known for their shyness and secrecy."

"So you think Ira's been waging a silent war against you for the last month?"

"Yeah, and what gets me is you, my best friend, seem to think I deserve it."

Nomura grimaces. "Look, only somebody with a serious imbalance would do this. And if it does actually turn out to be Ira, yeah, this is unforgivable. All I'm saying is, it didn't come completely out of nowhere."

As we leave the bathroom, Nomura and I still in full heated discussion, I nearly run over Mrs. Eagleton, the headmistress. "Mr. Schrader, we need to chat," she says. Eagleton looks as grisly and humorless as a prison warden. Not someone you want to encounter in normal circumstances, and definitely not somebody you want to "chat" with after the publication of a viral video in which you look like a member of the KKK.

"Come on, Alex," she says. "Follow me."

"But I've got to get to English. I have a paper due." Hey, you can't blame a guy for trying.

"Well, you'll have to make it up, then. Mrs. Terraciano will understand." Eagleton's already walking toward her office. "Well, come on, Mr. Schrader. I don't have all day."

30

My Secret

Haitian, Haitian, go back to your nation," Jenna chants (again! Can't she think of anything new?) as she and Angela pass me, Mary Agnes, and Maricel on our way to the Clark Street station a few minutes after school on Thursday.

I keep my mouth shut. Nothing good can come from responding to a crazy person, and my week has been bad enough already.

"I guess even Alex wants you to go back to your nation now, eh, Haitian girl?" Jenna asks. She and Angela turn around now, blocking our path. We're right in front of St. Christopher's, which I suppose is Jenna's idea of the perfect place to have a fight. "Nobody wants anything to do with you at all." *Except your annoying boyfriend*, I think.

Everyone in school has seen the video by now, and there's no way for me to feel any more embarrassed or stupid than I already do. So what does Jenna want now? Doesn't she have anything better to do? Mary Agnes and Maricel come to the edge of what is now a small circle, watching this confrontation between Jenna and me. The smirking Angela is here, too, showing her fool friend support.

"Why are you doing this, Jenna?" I ask. *Because I'm new? Because I wouldn't be your friend? Because your boyfriend likes me more than you?*

"There doesn't need to be a why. Because . . . I just don't like you, that's why."

"Let me ask you a question," I say. "Where is *your* family from? Because you have a West Indian look, don't you?"

"I'm Bushwick born and bred, girl," Jenna says. "They don't make 'em more Brooklyn than me."

"So you are, what, a Native American, then? Your ancestors were here before George Washington?"

This is going to be easy. Jenna Minaya may be mean, but she doesn't have the brains God gave a cow.

"*Mis padres* come from the Dominican," Jenna says. "And being Dominican's something to be proud of. We've got beautiful beaches that celebrities go to. We have our own celebrities, too. Best baseball players in the world come from the DR. It's not like Haiti over there, with nasty shantytowns and vodou dolls and people dying of crazy diseases."

I notice that a few girls have gathered around Angela. I suppose they want a front-row seat, where they can see all the action.

"I didn't live in a shantytown, Jenna. I lived in a villa. And Maman and I had a servant there, a sixteen-year-old Dominican girl called Blanca. She doesn't speak very good French, or Kreyol, but she's very sweet. She looks a little like you, actually."

"You're saying I remind you of your *maid*?"

"Yes, there's quite a resemblance, especially around the eyes. She's prettier, though, and more intelligent. We used to give her a nice big bonus every year, when we'd send her back to her parents." I tilt my head to the side and pause for effect because I'm enjoying this. Enjoying it more than I should be, considering how many more important things are happening right now in my life than my fight with this silly girl. But I can't help it; with all the hurt I'm feeling right now, why not share a little of it with her?

"Hey, maybe your parents are friends with hers?" I ask. "Maybe they all grew up together, in the slums."

"Ooooh," the crowd of girls moan, including Angela (so much for loyalty). If this were a boxing match—and perhaps it is—Jenna would be bleeding from her mouth, her nose, her eyes.

But I still haven't delivered my knockout punch. "Why don't you be a good girl," I say, "and go get me a tub to wash my feet." When she does nothing but stand there with her jaw hanging open, I say, "Go on! When I tell you to move, you move!"

Jenna Minaya does not move an inch. She closes her stupid, gaping mouth and narrows her eyes. Then she smiles: a sick, satisfied smile as if she, not I, is the one in control. She looks as strong as ever, more confident than a girl should be after what I've said to her.

"Bijou, about that villa you supposedly lived in with your precious maman," she says. "Who lives there now?"

I don't say anything. It's not a question she wants me to answer, anyway. She's going in for her own knockout blow now.

Out of the corner of my eye, I see others watching this showdown: Rocky, Trevor, Nomura, and even, at the far edges of the circle, him. *Get out of here, Alex*, I want to scream. *Leave me alone, forever!* I hate him for seeing this.

"Nobody does, right, Bijou?" Jenna asks. "Because while you've been running around here for the last two months talking about 'Maman this' and 'Maman that,' she died in the earthquake, didn't she? And your old grandfather was getting too sick and old to take care of you anymore.

"You didn't know I knew that, did you? I heard my mom talking about it on the phone, weeks ago. She's the parent rep on the board this year, so she knows all about you."

"You're a liar," says Mary Agnes, stepping from the edge of the circle and pointing her finger in Jenna's face. "And you'd better shut your mouth right now."

"My mom told me to keep quiet about it," Jenna says. "But I don't see why everybody shouldn't know the truth."

"Don't do this, Jenna," Mary Agnes says. "Just stop."

"At first, I actually felt sorry for you. I tried to be friends with you, but you were so *rude* to me." Then she turns to Angela and says, "Except for Maricel and Mary Agnes, who don't even count, Bijou has barely spoken a word to any of us. Am I right?"

No one says a thing, even Mary Agnes. Even me.

I want to yell at her, to fight back. But I feel like I'm in the middle of a nightmare, the kind where you try to scream, but not a sound comes from your mouth.

"But now that you've been here for over two months," Jenna says, "you should get real and admit it: you don't have a maman. Not anymore, anyway, and not ever again. So stop pretending, okay?"

"That is so weird," Angela says. "This whole time, she was trying to fool us? Why not just be honest?"

I say nothing. What is there to say? I can never hurt Jenna the way she has just hurt me. She has not seen enough of life to feel this kind of pain.

That is when I fall. Not a loud smack on the sidewalk concrete, but a soft crumble into the arms of Mary Agnes. I see Maman, as she was the last time I saw her, early on the morning of January 12, 2010. She looked me in the eyes, nuzzled my nose with hers, kissed me, and said, *"À bientôt."* *See you later.*

But later never came.

Mary Agnes and someone else, someone taller, help me to my feet. The crowd parts, letting us pass. Jenna looks at me one last time, no longer hateful. Angry. Sad. About to cry.

But why? Is she so filled with hate, she can't enjoy her victory for even a moment?

31

Strange Silence

Yes, I took the videos, and yes, they were uploaded to my YouTube account," Ira says to a blank-faced Mrs. Eagleton. "But I didn't edit them. And I didn't upload them, either."

"Then who did?" Eagleton asks. Ira is silent. And of course, so am I. "It's unlikely that Mr. Schrader would, given that everything he said violates the ethics code. What exactly were you thinking, Alex? This is not what we stand for at St. Chris's. And honestly, we'll be lucky if my colleagues at St. Catherine's don't cancel the Musicale *and* the final dance of the school year."

Great. One more reason for the entire population of both schools to hate me.

Eagleton is staring me down, and I don't know where to begin. I'm thinking more about what not to admit, and whom not to rat on, than how to explain this disaster away. And Ira is as tight-lipped as I am. Does that mean he really didn't upload the video, though? It's hard to imagine him doing it, but Nomura thinks Ira was right to be mad at me. The question is: Is Ira mad-mad, or wacko-mad?

"Well?" she asks. "Neither of you has *anything* to say for yourself?"

"It was a joke," I say. "I didn't mean for those things to sound the way they did, and I definitely didn't mean for them to wind up on the Internet."

"A joke?" Eagleton asks, astounded. "I'm not going to dignify some of the words you used by repeating them, but I do hope you realize that way of thinking, and of express-ing yourself, is no laughing matter."

"I know that now, ma'am. And I'm really, really sorry."

"I'm sorry, too," says Ira. "I don't know who took my camera, or why, but I'll find out." I kick Ira's shin, invisible under Eagleton's desk, and he chokes a cry of pain.

"Well, I'll be looking into that issue myself, rest assured," she says. "And as for the two of you, I'll be plac-ing a call to your parents to explain the situation. They have to know, of course. And while I will not be suspending you—the last thing you deserve is a vacation from your classes—you will not be permitted to participate in Musi-cale, or the dance." She gives one last sorrowful shake of her head. "If either event does indeed take place.

"All right," she finishes, waving us away like houseflies. "Off with you. Back to class."

· · · · ·

We turn a corner and get into every subject we weren't able to cover in Eagleton's office.

"I've been trying to tell you, but you've been impossible to get hold of," Ira says. "On Tuesday, somebody broke into my locker and ripped off my camera. By Wednesday morning, it had been returned, but this new video, the edited one that went on YouTube, was on it."

"Ira, you said you were going to delete it." I try to remember back to the movie, right after we'd left the bathroom. Hadn't he erased it then?

"I did, I swear. They must have looked in the trash . . . Rocky and Trevor."

"So you know it was them?"

"Who else would it be?"

"And what about that footage of me and Bijou holding hands?" I almost shove him but think better of it. One of the few things that could make this worse would be a second visit to Eagleton's. "What was that about?"

"I don't know," Ira says. "I was mad at you at the time— you were being a real jerk that day—but that's not why I shot it. I shot it because *Terror Lake* was lame, and I was bored. But I wasn't going to *do* anything with it. And I didn't think anybody else would, either. I have hundreds of random videos of people doing all kinds of meaningless stuff."

"That's pretty weird, Ira."

He shrugs, helpless. "If I'd realized something like this could happen, I never would have left my camera lying around like that."

"Wait," I say. "Did you say *hundreds* of random videos?"

"Yeah," Ira says, confused. "Why?"

Ira and I are just forming the beginnings of a revenge plan when we see Bijou and Jenna Minaya circling each other in front of St. Chris's. And I literally mean *circling*, like gladiators in the ring. At first, I can't even follow the conversation. Something about Dominican maids and Haitian villas. I have no idea what they're talking about, but I can practically see steam coming out of their nostrils. This is not going to be pretty.

At least I get why Bijou *still* hasn't written me back. If this girl fight is any indication, she's got plenty of other stuff on her mind right now.

When Jenna says that Bijou's mother is dead, that Bijou's been pretending, at first I don't believe a word of it. There's no way, I think, that she could have kept that a secret, especially from nosy Mary Agnes.

But then Mary Agnes gets right up in Jenna's face.

"You're a liar," she says, almost screaming. "And you'd better shut your mouth right now."

Jenna doesn't even try to deny it. She doesn't need to, I realize, because she's telling the truth. I can see it all over Bijou's face: the stunned, helpless look of someone whose last secret has been uncovered, someone who finally has nothing left to hide.

And I feel ashamed. Ashamed for not knowing before, and ashamed for knowing now. And ashamed for caring so much about whether Bijou liked me that I couldn't see how much pain she was in.

Then she faints, and Mary Agnes does an amazing job cushioning the fall. But Bijou's too heavy for her to handle alone, and she struggles to keep her upright. Before I have time to consider that I'm probably the last person Bijou would want by her side right now, I rush toward her.

But somebody beats me to it: Trevor.

I'm only a step or two away from Bijou when he puts his right arm up to block my path, then slyly slides his left arm around Bijou's waist. Then he helps Mary Agnes, who seems too focused on helping her friend to object to Trevor's gallant-seeming move, to carry Bijou up the steps and into school.

Really? Trevor? If it had to be a guy, couldn't it have been Nomura, or Ira, or anyone but him?

What's even harder to believe is that Bijou seems to actually like him being there. She certainly doesn't push him away, anyway, and before they're even halfway up the steps, she lets her head fall on his shoulder. What, are they going to be a couple now? Are my chances with the best girl I've ever known totally over because Trevor Zelo beat me to her side by a half second?

But if I'm devastated, at least I'm quiet about it. Jenna, on the other hand, is absolutely beside herself. After Trevor and Mary Agnes disappear with Bijou, she lets out a hoarse shriek and, after that, starts crying hysterically. She's like a human puddle, her chest heaving sobs. I never would have thought somebody as mean as Jenna Minaya could break down so completely.

And then it hits me: Jenna wrote the notes. The whole time, I'd been looking for a guy, but it was Jenna all along.

I sneak away before Nomura or Ira approaches me and manage to catch the subway before any of the other kids who witnessed the scene reach the platform. And I realize I've been doing it again, thinking about Trevor being closer to Bijou than I am, about Mary Agnes being closer to Bijou than I am. I've got to stop thinking so much about myself all the time. If I'm ever going to be friends with her again, I need to learn how to think about Bijou without always sticking myself into the equation.

The whole way home, I think about Bijou and her mom, and the strange silences that always seemed to follow the word "maman." The way Bijou got quiet whenever I asked about her mother. The faraway look in her eyes every time Port-au-Prince was mentioned. Maybe I didn't want to see how sad she truly was. At least now, I'm doing just that: *seeing*.

My mom told me that Bijou might have post-traumatic stress disorder and that there might be things about her experience that I wouldn't be able to understand. Maybe it's time to admit she might have been right about that one after all.

Mom also told me there's no difference between lying and omitting the truth. But in Bijou's case, there must be. I try to imagine what it might have been like if I'd lost Mom, then been sent to an entirely new country after my grandparents had gotten too old to take care of me. Would my mother's death have been something I'd want to discuss with a bunch of kids I'd only just met?

No, if I'd been in Bijou's shoes, I would have stuck with the strange silences, too.

32

A Boy in My Life

Pierre and Marie Claire haven't said a word about it, but I know it must have been Headmistress O'Biden who called a few minutes after dinner. After Tonton Pierre hung up, I could hear them from my room while I tried and failed to concentrate on my homework. Have you ever noticed how loud a whisper can be? It must be the least secretive way to have a conversation, like saying to anyone in the house, *Put your ear to the door and listen hard to every word we say.*

I hear only broken phrases from the living room.

Marie Claire: "What video? What boy?"

Pierre: ". . . send her to a girls school, and all they do is put them with boys? . . . not what I pay good money for . . ."

Marie Claire: ". . . the girl misses her mother . . . only natural . . ."

Pierre: ". . . and what business is it of these children whether she's alive or dead . . ."

That's when Pierre begins to cry. Without seeing it, I can picture what is happening. Marie Claire is kneeling now, by the chair her husband spends half his life sitting in. She is hugging him, comforting him.

I haven't cried in front of them. Not once since I arrived. My memories are my only comfort.

············ ℓℓℓℓℓ ············

And now, a knock on the door. Marie Claire checking on me, asking if I need anything, a little something to eat, though we finished a large meal of malanga only an hour ago. *Is your homework going okay? Do you need any help on it?* Neither my aunt nor my uncle has ever offered to help me with homework. They did not go to school in this country, so how could they?

I tell her, *No, I'm fine, Auntie*, and she takes my chin in her hand, kisses my forehead. *I know*, she says wordlessly. *I know you are fine.*

The matter will never be discussed openly between us. That's not the way things are done in our family. Pierre and Marie Claire will treat me very gently for a few days, and then, hopefully, they will forget about it.

And so will I. You see, having people find out about Maman is not the worst thing that has ever happened to me.

It is not even close.

············ ℓℓℓℓℓ ············

Doucet. Maman's name, and mine, too.

When friends and relatives of my mother meet me for the first time, they are so surprised by our likeness, they do not know quite what to say. They take a step back and hold a hand over their heart.

Doucet. It comes from the French word for "gentle." The French word for "sweet."

They say that I act like her, too. That I think before I speak, that I am careful and precise. We are the sweet ones in the family, the kind ones, the ones with the delicate features; everyone says it's true.

But they did not know Maman like I knew Maman. And they do not know how strong we can be. Strong as stone. Tough as leather. Prickly as barbed wire.

Maman knew how to survive. I am her daughter, and I know, too.

My uncle falls asleep in his chair most nights. As the weeks and months and years without Maman have passed, he still does not know what to say. But I don't blame him.

Maybe my likeness to Maman is the reason he never wants to let me out of his sight. Maybe the pain is too great. Maybe he is just tired of missing her.

It's different for me, though. If I didn't have the few photographs that I keep in the drawer next to my bed, I'm not sure I would remember what she looked like at all. My memories of her are fading, too, like those images worn thin from too much touching. Smells, feelings . . . I remember those. But the memories of her face, her expressions, were the first to go. The woman in the photos looks like half a stranger now.

Until I look in the mirror, and remember.

Maybe that's why I refuse to talk about Maman in the past tense.

Because I see her every day, first thing in the morning, staring me right in the face.

......———ℓℓℓℓℓ———...

"Are you sure there's no way for me to convince you to come to rehearsal tomorrow?" Mary Agnes asks. We're riding the 2 train on a Tuesday, after school, grasping a portion of the cold steel pole that stands in the middle of the subway car like a leafless winter tree. "You know, he won't even be there."

I have refused to let her even speak Alex's name for a week. And thankfully, I haven't had to see him myself. He has been forbidden from participating in Musicale.

"Thank you for asking," I say. "I do appreciate it, really. But I would rather just watch, okay?"

"Listen, Bijou, I know you don't want to talk about him, and I hear you," Mary Agnes says with extra care. "But let me say this. If he has anything to say about the video, any explanation, you should at least hear him out."

"You forgot to say, 'You owe him that much,'" I say.

"You don't owe him *anything*." She pulls her gum out of her mouth and places it delicately in a napkin. "But maybe you owe it to yourself."

"What does that mean?"

"Look, Bijou, I consider you a friend. And I hope you think of me as one, too, even though we're pretty different. But maybe you could use more than one friend. And Alex? No matter what it seems like he did, he's the kind of boy you want in your life. Believe me."

My answer is a smile and a shrug; that is all I can give her right now.

"Talk to him, okay? See what he has to say for himself."

"I will think about it," I say as Mary Agnes struggles to pull on her backpack that probably weighs half what she does. "And Mary Agnes, you *are* my friend. Thank you, okay?" She might be bossy, she might be silly at times, but I know a friend when I see one.

"Of course, sweetie, of course." I kiss her twice on her cheeks, a gesture she is finally growing used to after these nearly three months with me.

Alone now, transferring to the Q train, I wonder, is Alex the kind of boy I want in my life?

I have been in America for only twelve weeks. I survived the biggest earthquake in the history of my country, and the death of the person closest to me in the world. I am surviving Brooklyn, its strange people, its confusing rules, its freezing weather, its dirty subway platforms. And I am fine.

So why would I need a boy in my life at all?

Dear Alex,

I had a good talk with Mary Agnes today, and I do understand that you were not trying to be mean. And that nothing that happened was actually even your fault. I know you are not a bad person and that you would never try to hurt me on purpose.

But I do think that we come from very, very different places and have had very different lives. People in America like to pretend that that doesn't matter, but I believe it does.

I like you, Alex, and you've told me you like me, too. For a moment, I was beginning to think that that was enough. But now I've found out—I've learned the hard way—that it's not.

I'm sorry, Alex. I know you want to get to know me better. You want to be close friends. But for me, right now, this is not possible.

I'll see you . . . sometime.

Bijou

 33

Preparations

Ira wasn't kidding. He has hundreds, if not thousands, of hours of video on his laptop. And I'd be surprised if he didn't have footage of nearly every member of the St. Cathopher's family. Since I'm still big-time grounded, he's over at my house, and we're scouring his computer for suitable "gotcha" material.

"You could nail every kid we know," I say, shaking my head.

"Every teacher, too." He smiles.

We've only been searching his library for five minutes, and already I've seen: a fifth-grade Greg Vargas wetting his pants during a handball game; Mr. Miller leaving the john without washing his hands; even Angela Gudrun, obviously unaccustomed to her fancy high heels, taking a nasty spill at Spring Fling.

"Is this mostly hidden-camera stuff, or what?"

"The Mr. Miller one in the bathroom? Yeah. But that was just an experiment. Mostly, though, I just walk around with the camera. When something interesting happens, I just keep it at my waist and press record. See, no start-up noise whatsoever."

"Uh, yeah, I noticed." It's hard not to remember one of the more recent occasions when Ira used this keep-it-at-the-waist-and-press-record method.

"Alex, really, I'm sorry. I never—"

"What's done is done," I say. While it's tempting to get mad at him all over again, I try to focus on the present. "I know you never would have put it out in the world on your own, and you couldn't have predicted that Rocky and Trevor would steal it."

"Yeah, but now I know how to handle security better. I used to leave videos on the camera for a few days at a time before uploading them to my computer. But I'll never do that again. The videos go straight to my laptop, and the laptop stays far away from school."

We check out some more videos. The wide-scale embarrassment potential is epic, but Ira hasn't named the files or organized them in any way, so locating stuff on our specific targets is tricky, to say the least.

"One question," I say. "Why do you do this?"

"Well, you know I want to be a director one day,

right? But it's not only that. It's the weird stuff people do when they think nobody's looking at them. I find it . . . fascinating."

"And you really shoot all this stuff without anybody noticing you?"

"The time in the bathroom with you was the only time somebody caught me in the act."

"That's nuts. I mean, I get it, the camera's at your waist, not balancing on your shoulder, but still . . . it's not *that* hard to notice."

"The camera's not hard to notice, but I am."

"Huh?"

He thinks for a second. "As soon as our entire class became completely obsessed with girls—which happened pretty much overnight, with zero warning—it was like I became invisible. Not just to girls, but to my friends, too."

"That's so untrue." It is, isn't it?

"Oh, come on, Alex. Take Spring Fling as an example. You basically told me to get lost as soon as the girls came over. Go talk to the geeks, you said."

"I did not," I say, my stomach churning. I, Alex Schrader, may be a wee bit selfish at times, but I didn't abandon one of my oldest friends as soon as I became interested in girls. Or did I?

" 'Friendship can walk the plank, matey,' right?"

Wow, he remembers that line as well as Nomura does.

"Okay, we've both done some stupid things in the last five weeks," I say. "Truce?" I know a bro-shake won't make up for my behavior, but hopefully it's a start.

"Truce," Ira says. We squeeze wrists and go through the elaborate handshake that Nomura concocted when the three of us were eleven. We still remember every last grip, every sweet little palm slide, ending on a down-low clasp that's way slicker and slier than the jocky high fives of Rocky and Trevor.

"Okay, so we've at least got some time stamps to work with here," I say, turning my attention to the file folder on Ira's laptop again.

"That, we do."

"Let's stick with the night of Spring Fling."

Ira chuckles wickedly and rubs his hands together. "You thinking what I'm thinking?" he asks.

"I do believe we're on the same page."

But before we can find what we're looking for, I hear a key turning in our front-door lock. I look at my watch. It's already five fifteen! Dolly and my mom aren't supposed to be here, not yet, but Ira *definitely* isn't. Not while I'm grounded.

"Hello?" I call, trying for a friendly tone. I pray it's only Dolly.

"Hi," two voices call. Ugh. My mom's with her. Dolly's cello must have needed a ride somewhere, so Mom provided it. If I'm going to pull this off, I'll need to keep better tabs on their schedules.

"Should I hide?" Ira asks.

"No," I say. "I'll tell her we're working on a project." I give a sad laugh. "After all, how much more grounded can I be than I already am?"

…… ℓℓℓℓℓ ……

After Ira leaves, I wonder if hiding him might have been a better strategy.

"So what's this video project about?" Mom asks, having finally calmed down about Ira's being here at all. I'm downstairs now, talking to her while she puts away her coat and her briefcase, and she seems to have accepted the fact that I couldn't tell her about the "assignment" Ira and I were working on, because I don't have a phone.

"It's for this human-behavior project," I say. I don't know where I come up with this stuff, but it's not a flat-out lie (I'm back into "omitting the truth" territory, I guess). We *are*, in fact, doing a human-behavior project; it just happens to be completely extracurricular.

"After Mrs. Eagleton's phone call," she says, "the last thing I want to see in this house is you and Ira hunched over a laptop and a video camera."

"This is important," I say. "You'll see."

"More or less important than your incessant practicing

on that idiotic drum?" Dolly breaks in, as if anyone had asked for her opinion, nodding toward the rada standing discreetly in the corner of the room.

"Nine times out of ten, I'm done practicing by the time you get home." Mom outlawed any contact with Bijou or her rhythm-virtuoso brother, but she did give in after I begged her to let me stick with my practice routine during my grounding. I guess she doesn't have the heart to make me give up the one thing I've ever been halfway good at.

"Yeah, it's that one time out of ten I'm concerned with."

"You know how many *thousands* of times I've lost sleep 'cause of that plank of wood *you're* constantly screeching away on?"

"Kids, please," Mom says. "The last thing I need at the end of the day is to hear the two of you bickering."

Behind Mom's back, I stick my tongue out at my obnoxious sister. In the last week, I've lost my phone, my freedom, and the first girl I've ever liked. I'm not going to let Dolly take away my rada, too.

—— ♪♪♪♪ ——

"Hey, Alex. Haven't heard from you in a few days," Jou Jou says, sounding genuinely happy to hear from me, as opposed to coldly suspicious of a kid who recently humiliated his sister (even if he didn't mean to). Could Bijou possibly not have told him? "I was starting to get worried, man. Everything cool?"

"Yeah, yeah, fine," I say. And, figuring it's better to come out with it, I take a chance. "Although I don't know if everything's cool between your sister and me."

Jou Jou can't see me, but I'm cringing like I'm about to receive a blow. I'm taking a risk here by even bringing up the issue of the video; if he knows there's something wrong between me and Bijou, all trust between the two of us will evaporate instantly. Because blood is thicker than . . . cow skin. Right?

He takes a while to answer. "Listen, Alex, Bijou don't tell me anything about this, and my aunt and uncle didn't say nothing, either. But I think if you and I are gonna keep going with the lessons, you'd better tell me what's going on."

So I do. I tell him everything about the video, about Rocky and Trevor, and about how I plan to get them back. And I tell him about how Bijou was the unintended victim of Rocky and Trevor's stupidity, and Ira's, and mine. I even tell him about the letter I finally (!) got from Bijou, figuring that if I leave out even a single detail and he finds out later, I'll look like a jerk. *(Okay, Mom, I guess I'm starting to see how "omitting the truth" really isn't the way to go, after all.)* I tell him that I understand why Bijou wants to push the pause button on our friendship, but that, for now, anyway, I still don't want to take no for an answer.

"This is bad," Jou Jou says. "I can see how it happened, but I wish it hadn't happened to her, you know? She's the last person in the world who deserves it."

"Believe me, I know," I say. "It sucks. It's been . . . a nightmare."

Then, I tell Jou Jou about how I plan to get Bijou back, too. About what she means to me, and how I have to try to win her friendship back one last time. I won't be able to do it without his help, after all.

"Alex, you did say she wrote you and said she didn't want to see you anymore, am I right?"

"Well, yeah, but—"

"And you still think it's a good idea to keep pushing like this? What if she's right?"

"Listen, if this doesn't work, I will never so much as look at Bijou again. I will leave her completely in peace and not have a problem with it." I have to pause for a second, because the idea of never even getting to talk to Bijou again makes me all emotional. "I can't explain it, but I . . . need to do this."

Jou Jou takes a deep breath. "Alex, you've got a sister, am I right?"

"Yeah. Dolly."

"Okay, Dolly. Try to imagine if somebody you had only known for a few weeks came to *you* with a plan like this in mind. Would you trust that person?"

I don't know what to say. Obviously, he's got a serious point here.

"Bijou is all I've got, Alex. She's the most important person in the world to me."

"I know. . . . I'm sure she is. I'm really sorry I even—"

"I can really trust you, you're saying?"

"Yes," I tell him. "I swear it."

"Okay, Alex, I'm in."

"That's awesome! But you won't tell her we're . . . collaborating?"

"No, man. It won't work if I let the secret out now, will it?" He pauses. "But I'm putting my trust in you, Alex. You understand what that means, right?"

"I do. And I won't let you down. Promise."

"And you'd *better* be practicing your raboday pattern, man. Because it won't work unless you're sounding tight. Got it?"

"I'll be ready," I say.

34

Musicale

Performing in Musicale may not be mandatory, but everyone is required to attend. Of course, getting up on the stage to perform did not seem appealing to me at all, not after I have already provided so much entertainment to both schools (live and on film, which makes me a multimedia sensation).

But now I'm here, sitting in the bleachers of the gymnasium, the same one where I met Alex only a month ago, with Pierre and Marie Claire to my left, waiting for the performance to begin. And I realize that just watching might be even worse. At least if I were performing, I would be too nervous preparing to remember the truth: that my life in Brooklyn has only gone from bad to worse.

I watch as the bleachers begin to fill. While I am not the only one with family here—even though it is only

three o'clock, many parents are; *that* is how seriously
Musicale is taken in these schools—I am quite sure I'm the
only one whose aunt and uncle have come for the sole purpose of making sure that I stay away from boys, and that
they stay away from me. My uncle deliberately chose the
last row of seats, farthest away from the stage, even though
we arrived so early that there were plenty of better seats
still available.

"How long is this going to last?" Tonton Pierre says,
shifting his weight on the uncomfortable aluminum seat.

It's been a week since the video showed up and my fight
with Jenna, but my problems at school are still a big topic
at home. Tonton Pierre was surprisingly gentle toward me
for the first day or two, but then he started to ask me questions: How did I come to know the boys in the video? Why
was that mean girl so jealous of me? Why was I associating
with such misguided young people? And when he found out
that I had joined a Musicale group that included boys, he
became so angry that Marie Claire had to step between us
and tell her husband to calm down, take a breath, and stop
berating his niece.

Marie Claire pats Pierre on the knee. "Sit back and
relax, *mon cher.* We are here, at Bijou's school. And we are
going to enjoy the performance."

Tonton Pierre grumbles and shrugs, as if accepting a
brief sentence in prison.

The bleachers are starting to fill up. Nomura leads his parents into the third row, then jogs backstage. Maricel is right behind him, although I don't see Ira. Rocky, his hair slick and shiny, walks ten feet in front of his parents and scowls at his balding father. Jenna is here, too, with her mother and little brother. I shrink into my skin, wanting to avoid any contact with her. The last thing I need is for Pierre to realize who she is and create a scene. And I doubt her mama would be any more pleased to see me, the girl who had called her daughter a common house servant.

Mary Agnes looks up, finds me, gives me a wave. She is leading her parents and three younger siblings—every one of them with carrot-colored hair and milky, freckled skin that wouldn't survive a day in Port-au-Prince—into front-row seats, which are permanently reserved for her, since she is on the planning committee for every event in the school's calendar. I wave back, smile, and hope that Mary Agnes doesn't feel a sentimental urge to introduce herself to *La Famille* Doucet.

But it is too late. Here she comes, marching up the steps with a neon smile.

"Hi, Bijou!" She kisses me on both cheeks, then says, "Hello, Mr. and Mrs. Doucet, I'm Mary Agnes Brady," and extends her hand as if she has come to my house to take me to the high school prom (no, we don't have prom in Haiti, and yes, I learned what prom is on *Tous Mes Enfants*).

Is she unaware of the awkwardness of the situation, or does she simply not care? I brace myself for Pierre's reaction, but he and Marie Claire both return Mary Agnes's greeting politely.

"I wanted to tell you both how much we all love Bijou here at St. Catherine's," she says, more like a headmistress now than a prom date.

"Oh, really?" says Pierre.

Marie Claire squeezes his thigh. And not with love. It's an order: *Don't cause trouble.*

"Well, I'm really glad she came here," Mary Agnes says, "and that we've become friends."

Mary Agnes doesn't stop there. In less than three minutes, she manages to tell us about herself and her family and to get more information on my uncle and his furniture-restoration business, on Marie Claire's part-time job as an administrator at Kings County Hospital, than I knew myself. Pierre and Marie Claire nod and smile, and Pierre even asks some questions of his own. He wants to know, for some reason, how long she has lived in Park Slope, what her parents do for a living, even the names of her siblings. She tells him, and he seems as fascinated as if she were providing the explanation to the origin of life.

Mary Agnes checks her watch. "Oops, I'm really sorry, I need to get going," she says. "It was *so* nice to meet you." And she hugs them. Both of them! "Bijou, are you sure I can't change your mind? You'd dance circles around Maricel and me."

"I'm fine here," I say, smiling. "Really."

"Are you sure, Bijou?" my uncle asks.

I look at him as if he is a madman. As if he has asked me to change into a swimsuit and do cartwheels in front of everyone. "No, Uncle," I say. "I really am fine." Marie Claire laughs into her palm.

"Okay, I had to try," Mary Agnes says. And just like that, as the lights go down, she leaves us, waves to her family, and disappears behind the stage.

"What just happened?" Marie Claire asks.

"We just met . . . a very nice girl," Pierre says. "A very impressive young lady."

Yesterday, Mary Agnes was a central part of the conspiracy to involve me in a sinful coeducational Musicale performance, and now she is my uncle's favorite seventh grader in Brooklyn. Either I don't know Pierre as well as I thought, or when Mary Agnes grows up, she should be an ambassador for world peace.

The lights have gone out completely now, and a single spotlight shows on the podium. Headmistress O'Biden welcomes us all to this year's St. Catherine's–St. Christopher's Intramural Spring Musicale. Everyone applauds and cheers, and within moments, the first act, an eighth-grade boy and girl duo, are singing "Falling Slowly," from the musical *Once*. It is a pretty song, and as singers, they are not bad. Marie Claire brings out a tissue to wipe away a tear at the corner of her eye while Pierre checks his watch for the hundredth time.

As Jenna and Angela take the stage as the second act, wearing matching short skirts and fishnet stockings, my whole body stiffens. I try to tell myself there is no way that they will try to embarrass me, not today, not ever again. But it is only as they are nearly finished with their number, a "sexy" but harmless dance routine set to the song "California Gurls" that I allow myself to relax.

"Silly," Pierre says too loudly while the boys around us hoot and holler. "Their outfits aren't appropriate, and they should be more . . . dignified." Marie Claire gives him a look, but I could not have said it better myself.

"Thank you very much, girls," says Headmistress O'Biden, who is probably relieved herself that Angela and Jenna did not push any more boundaries than they did. "Next, please welcome Mary Agnes Brady, John Nomura, and Maricel and Ira Lopez. Their choice of song isn't listed here, but I'm sure they have something very special in store for us." Half the audience claps; others giggle and cheer sarcastically.

Ira appears onstage alone and puts his laptop on a table, fiddling with cords and wires. He is probably getting the backing track ready. In the only rehearsal I attended, we didn't even succeed in picking a song, so I have no idea what they decided on in the end. He is also probably preparing some sort of video, although I pray that the boy is a bit better organized now. Mary Agnes must have been crazy, after everything that's happened, to allow him to be responsible for any kind of visual entertainment.

Ira is still monkeying with his machine and talking to the man running the sound and video system, but he keeps looking off to the side of the stage. He tries to concentrate on his work, but someone is obviously distracting him.

Alex walks onto the stage and cups his hand over Ira's ear.

"Who is that?" Pierre asks. I ignore him and lean forward in my seat.

Ira is shaking his head, *no, no.*

"What's happening?" Marie Claire asks. "Are they having some kind of technical problem?" I pray the problem is only technical.

"Who is that boy?" Pierre asks. I'm wondering what special gift of intuition my uncle possesses that could draw his attention to Alex Schrader.

Now Rocky and Trevor are on the stage, too, and Alex is gone. Ira unplugs one of the wires he connected only a moment earlier, and apparently plays something for the two of them, who hunch over the machine with great interest. Rocky puts his hand over his mouth, looking surprised, and Trevor, who I haven't seen since that strange moment when he insisted on helping Mary Agnes carry me into school, rocks uncomfortably on his heels. Alex, checking their reaction, nods a quick *okay*, and all but pushes them off the stage.

When Alex returns, he is not alone. He is with his rada drum. And he is with my brother.

"Is that *Jou Jou?*" Marie Claire asks. "What is *he* doing here?"

"That's the boy," Pierre says, and he's not talking about my brother. "God help me, I *knew* that was the boy."

"Tonton, *je t'implores. Ne fais rien,*" I say. *Uncle, I beg you. Don't do anything.*

Now the headmistress is whispering to Alex. She looks confused. Or angry. Or both. But finally she gives him the microphone and walks to the side of the stage. Alex nods toward my brother, who starts to play the raboday rhythm, his right hand slapping the stick loudly on the cow-skin head and cupping the drum with warm bass tones with his left.

"The white boy is going to play rara music," Pierre murmurs, helpless. "God help us all."

Alex steps to the front of the stage and calls out to the audience over the ancient vodou rhythm.

"Ladies and gentlemen," he starts, "I'm really sorry to interrupt, but there's something I really need to say right now."

There is nervous laughter from the audience, and one boy yells, "Schrader, I need to say right now that you're a total dork!"

"I'm not talking to *all* of you," Alex says. "Just to one of you."

I fight the urge to cover my face with my hands.

"How about talking to *none* of us?" another boy says.

Then Trevor stands up and yells, "Everybody shut up and let Schrader talk!"

Rocky stands next to him, nodding. Suddenly they are all best friends? When the crowd quiets down, the two of them take their seats.

"The only person I want to talk to, the person who matters most to me in this entire room, is you, Bijou," he says.

Oh my Lord, Alex. *S'il te plaît, ne fais pas ça. Please, don't do this.*

Jou Jou's raboday goes even stronger and louder, but Alex is still able to call out above the rhythm, his voice a high, clear tenor. "Bijou, you are the best person, the truest person, in this room. And I would be so honored if you would join me right now and help us do this raboday right. We can't do it without you."

He cannot be serious. He cannot think that this is the right time, the right place, to declare his feelings for me. That is what he is doing, isn't it? This is more, after all, than asking me to dance along with the raboday.

Jou Jou yells above the beat, "Come on, Bijou! Get down here, sister!"

The people in the rows in front of us, each and every one of them, turn around to stare at me. I've never seen any of these parents, brothers, and sisters in my life. How do they even know I am the one he's talking to—can they feel the heat burning off my cheeks? (Alex has at last succeeded in making *me* blush.) The Lopezes, the Minayas, even the tiny, carrot-colored Brady children, are all staring at me, waiting for a decision.

"Go ahead, child," whispers Marie Claire. "Do it."

"Don't you dare," says Pierre. "I absolutely forbid it."

I look at the stage, tears filling my eyes. Do I want to go and dance up on that stage with this crazy boy? With this sweet boy who is also the most inappropriate person I have ever met?

Alex, I'm going to get you for this. And Jou Jou, you, too.

 35

Last-Minute Change of Plans

We can't do it, Ira," I whisper to him. I can already feel Eagleton staring daggers into my back and know that there's only a matter of seconds before I get yanked off the stage. But Jou Jou's waiting and ready to go, so if I'm going to pull this off, if I'm going to do this the right way, it's got to happen right now. And it's got to come off perfectly.

"What do you mean?" Ira thinks I'm a nut. He spent four hours putting together the most perfect video of his life, a video that would end the St. Cathopher's dominance of Rocky Van Sant and Trevor Zelo now and forevermore. And now I'm yanking that moment of supreme pleasure away from him. Then he spots R and T themselves, who are waiting nervously at the far end of the stage. "And what are *they* doing here?"

"If we show it to them, we've got them in the palm of our hands forever, and we don't get in any trouble. But if we do it, if we purposely humiliate them in public, then we'll be just like them."

Ira throws up his hands, exasperated. "What if, this once, I *want* to be like them?" he asks. "They get to do whatever they want around here. And they have hot girlfriends."

"Mr. Schrader, get off this stage right now," Eagleton hisses. "You're not even supposed to be here."

O'Biden is right beside her. "I'll handle this," she says, stepping up to the mic and telling the audience that the next act needs a few more seconds to prepare. For a quick second, I panic, the headmistress's presence reminding me that my mom is out there in the audience somewhere, surely wondering what the heck her rebellious, disobedient son is up to now. O'Biden is nodding toward the soundman, who gets the idea and puts a song on to chill everybody out. And I take it as a cue to chill out myself. I've gotten this far; now it's time to see this thing through.

I scramble to the side of the stage, and Rocky and Trevor join Ira. It wasn't hard to get them to follow me up to the stage. I told them we'd gotten hold of material that made the video they uploaded look like an episode of *iCarly*.

"Have you lost your mind, Schrader?" Rocky hissed, but Trevor could see how serious I was, and the two of them followed me up here, meek as lambs.

And they both get it as soon as they identify their own

pretty faces in the video. I'm kneeling, stage right, out of the headmistress's view, hopefully, but close enough to hear. I'm not going to miss a second of this; if all goes according to plan, it's going to be my shining moment.

"Wait, this is *not* hooked up to the main screen, right?" Trevor asks Ira, craning his neck up for a look above the stage and looking relieved to see that the only light up there is emanating from Ira's laptop (and possibly Rocky's bioluminescent hair goop).

The video isn't exactly what I would call original. It was directed by Ira and myself. But it was edited in the unmistakable style of Rocky and Trevor themselves. And this time, I definitely plagiarized on purpose.

In the video, Rocky, looking straight at Ira's "invisible" camera, says, "The two of us own this school. Every girl here wants to be with us; every guy here wants to be us. And that's never gonna change."

Then Trevor chimes in with "Amen to that!" and a swell of gospel music (a genius touch suggested by my codirector) bubbles away on the soundtrack. Trevor's voice gets louder and more echoey, repeating "Amen to that!" again and again and again, while Rocky comes back in with "Every girl here wants to be with us," repeating the egomaniacal phrase again and again.

Back in real time, Trevor says, "You were planning on showing this, but now you're not?"

"Exactly," I say.

"And how does that work, exactly?" Rocky asks.

"Because I don't need to. Because I know what it feels like to look like a complete idiot in front of the whole school, and it's not something I'd wish upon my worst enemies." It's hard not to smile as I add the obvious: "Even when they totally deserve it."

"What do you want in return, though?" Trevor asks.

I give Jou Jou the signal, thankful that I was able to get him through security as a member of the Doucet family, even though the Doucet family won't know he's on the premises for another ten or fifteen seconds. Jou Jou, smiling, passes me my rada, sits down, and starts up the raboday rhythm, loud and clear.

"All I want you to do right now is get off the stage," I say. "I've got more important things to do."

"Easy enough," Rocky says. "Later!" He bounds off, but Trevor is slower to leave.

"Oh," I tell him. "Next time you guys get the urge to humiliate me or any of my friends, you should probably know that Ira and I have literally *hours'* worth of material on you two that makes this thing look like a public-service announcement."

"Fine, man, fine," he says, walking away. Then, over his shoulder, "She liked you better, anyway. You're lucky." And he jumps into the darkness.

36

Why Can't We Be Friends?

Even as I squeeze out of the back row of the bleachers and down the steps to the gym floor—not an easy thing to do in the dark, even without three hundred people wondering who "Bijou" is, and what she is about to do—I have not decided whether to go to the stage or run to the exit sign to the safety of Pineapple Street. All I know is that I had to get out of that seat, sandwiched between my aunt and an uncle who forbade me from so much as moving.

All I knew was this: I needed the room to make a choice for myself.

Once I reach the floor, Alex is no longer standing at the edge of the stage, no longer calling for me to join him. He is seated next to Jou Jou on a plain metal chair, with the old, scratched-up rada in front of him, beating out the ancient vodou rhythm. The rhythm of my people. And through some miracle, he is actually good at it.

Like he was in the Rara Gran Bwa rehearsal and at his lesson, he is lost in the music, his eyes closed in concentration. And I don't know whether he means it like this or not, but in his focus on the drum, Alex seems to be saying to me, *I'm done trying to convince you; now you can make up your own mind.*

Headmistress O'Biden stands less than ten feet to the side, shaking her head at Alex and my brother, and I have to admit, it is a funny sight: this worried old lady, so frustrated by a lovesick boy and the nineteen-year-old Haitian he has brought into her school to bang out this crazy-seeming music. She doesn't know how to solve this rara problem, so she stands there, still as a statue.

Now that the stage and the exit sign are both twenty feet apart, I try to think about what Maman would do. Would she accept this sweet and handsome, yet absolutely embarrassing, boy's invitation? Would she exhibit herself to all her classmates, once more, in yet another moment sure to be captured on video? Or would she escape into her own quiet space again, away from these well-meaning but unpredictable new friends?

Maman was a fun, exciting person who loved to laugh and dance and sing—lighting up the world each and every

time she did—but she was also very private and had only a
few people in her life who truly knew her.

So again I'm thinking, *What would Maman do?*
Would she run to the stage or to the street?

Maman is not here, though. Only me. So, what would
Bijou do?

...——ℓℓℓℓℓ——...

The lights are so bright up here, I can see only Alex and Jou
Jou. I strike the small cowbell with the stick I found lying
next to my brother, playing the rhythm I have known by
heart my entire life, and it is impossible not to return his
smile.

Maman did choose the stage, I think.

She is here with us.

In Jou Jou.

In me.

And, just maybe, in Alex, too.

I dance to the raboday, and I don't need to think any
more about it than I think about striking the bell. As unex-
pected as it is to be introducing St. Catherine's to the world
of rara, the dance itself is the most natural thing in the
world. It works best when you're not trying at all, not even
thinking at all.

Before long, the audience is clapping, quite loudly, along
to the beat, and Ira has taken his position again behind the

laptop, with Maricel by his side. They're fiddling with something—I'm not sure what.

"What's that, about a hundred and ten beats per minute?" Maricel asks Alex, who shrugs in response, still lost in the music.

"No clue," he says, smiling, never losing the beat of the raboday.

"About a hundred and fifteen!" Jou Jou cries out. "What you got in mind?"

"Something cool," Ira says as he and Maricel continue to tinker.

Suddenly, Mary Agnes and Nomura appear at the edge of the stage, and before I know I am doing it, I pull them onto the stage with me.

"Ack!" Mary Agnes says. "Are you sure this is a good idea?"

"Yeah," Nomura says. "We can't dance Haitian."

"Just follow me," I say, demonstrating with arms, legs, and hips.

The crowd yells encouragement as the two of them start to copy my movements. And they're not bad!

"Woo!" Alex yells, and I smile back at him.

I will still get you back for this, I think. *But for now, this is fun.*

Meanwhile, Ira and Maricel are bobbing their heads up and down, sharing a pair of headphones like DJs. They exchange a look with Jou Jou, who is nodding along with them. "One . . . two . . . three . . . four!" my brother calls out to them.

And out of nowhere, a song comes booming out of the sound system, perfectly matching the raboday tempo.

"Yes!" Alex yells.

"Perfect!" Jou Jou adds a loud, fast drum fill, using both sticks on the rada now.

"What is this?" I ask Mary Agnes, who, flushed with the dancing, is red as an apple.

"It's a new mash-up, by DJ Riplo," Nomura says.

I wonder if this DJ Riplo maybe has some Haitian blood in him. "It's great," I yell. "What's it called?"

"It's called 'Why Can't We Be Friends?'!" Mary Agnes says, bringing me in close for a hug so tight I almost fall over. Nomura laughs so hard, his glasses fall off, and he scoops them up quickly before any of us enthusiastic dancers steps on them.

Alex and Jou Jou are trading fills now, soloing over the track that booms out across the gymnasium. In the crowd, I can see the shadowy outlines of parents and kids spilling from the bleachers to the floor. Everyone is dancing now, singing to the raboday.

Then, something funny happens. It is like I am watching a video, and someone has slowed everything down—the rhythm of the raboday, the motions of the dancers, even the spotlights that sweep across the stage—so that I can see every bit of movement in this enormous room, frame by frame. As if something, someone is telling me, *Bijou, pay attention. This is for you. Make sure not to miss anything.*

I turn around and smile toward my brother, but he is so into the music, he doesn't even notice. Alex, too, has his eyes closed, concentrating hard on the rhythm. Who ever thought I would meet an American boy who would have such a natural gift for rara music? It is like a small miracle.

Then Alex opens his eyes, notices me, and smiles. I cannot help but laugh, and Alex cannot, either. He leans his head back, looks from me to the ceiling and back, and shares this private moment with me. All the while, he never loses track of the raboday.

Looking out across the gym, I try to find Tonton Pierre and Auntie. The lights are so bright, there is no way for me to see them, even with this power I suddenly have, this ability to slow down time. Still, though, I know they are out there, somewhere, and that they must be enjoying this moment as much as I am. How could they not? A whole school—two schools!—dancing to the music of our people.

This is when I realize that the voice I'm hearing, the one telling me to watch, and notice, every single thing that is happening, urging me to store these details in my memory forever, belongs to Maman. She is the one helping me to see, and feel, and understand.

Maman is gone, but she is here.

In me. In my brother. In my aunt and uncle.

Maybe even, a little bit, in Alex.

"How awesome is this?" screams Mary Agnes.

"It's awesome!" I yell, using another American word I learned on *Tous Mes Enfants.* "Totally awesome!"

ACKNOWLEDGMENTS

I would like to thank Amy Ellenbogen, Toni Cela, Fabienne Doucet, Jeremy Robins, Lois Wilcken, Morgan Zwerlein, Gina Vellani, and everyone at the Church Avenue Merchants Block Association (CAMBA), my endlessly supportive agent Marissa Walsh, and two inspiring editors, Stacy Cantor Abrams and Mary Kate Castellani, whose insights surprised and delighted me, and made this book so much better.

AUTHOR'S NOTE

In 2007, I got a chance to see a great documentary film by my friend Jeremy Robins called *The Other Side of the Water: The Journey of a Haitian Rara Band in Brooklyn.* The movie tells the story of Djarara, a Flatbush, Brooklyn-based group that, over the last two decades, has revolutionized rara music in their adopted country, winning scores of American fans in the process.

At the time, I lived in Ditmas Park, Brooklyn—Alex's neighborhood in *A Song for Bijou*, just a stone's throw away from Flatbush. Watching the film, I was amazed that these great musicians were reinventing their culture less than a mile away from my house. How could something so exciting be happening almost literally in my backyard, without me knowing a thing about it? I didn't forget about Djarara. These musicians, their struggles and triumphs, stayed with me long after the lights came up and I walked out of the theater. (And while I didn't know it yet, the character of Jou Jou would be based on some of the young men I had "gotten to know" in the movie.)

Three years later, when the earthquake struck Haiti, millions around the world were spellbound by the tragedy.

And as I followed the story along with everyone else, I couldn't help but think of the tens of thousands of Haitians living right here in Brooklyn and the devastating impact the event must have had on their families back home.

I began to imagine the intersecting lives of Bijou, a strong and determined survivor of the quake, and Alex, a shy Brooklyn boy who can't possibly understand what Bijou has been through, but wants to try. There was no real story yet. All I had was an idea about a relationship between two seventh graders that survives despite peer pressure, cultural prejudices, and a hundred and one misunderstandings. And also, I had a title, *A Song for Bijou*. I'm not sure why, but the character name and the title came almost immediately. I didn't have a clue how this "song" would fit into the story, but I liked the sound of the title, and it stuck.

When it came to the actual story, it wasn't too tough to write from Alex's perspective. My own childhood was a bit like his—I grew up with a single mom until I was eleven, and I went to a school almost exactly like St. Christopher's (although we weren't lucky enough to have a sister school just a few blocks away!), so it wasn't difficult to imagine the mixture of admiration, respect, and confusion that Bijou would cause in him. But to be able to write from Bijou's point of view, I knew I'd need to spend some time with people who had lived a life similar to hers. Over the next few months, I spoke with Haitian and Haitian American women, eager to know about their experiences living and going to school in New York City.

Two of them, Toni Cela and Fabienne Doucet (who kindly allowed me to use her last name for Bijou), helped me to understand the experience of a newly arrived seventh-grade girl whose country and culture seem so often to be ignored, misunderstood, or feared. Both Toni and Fabienne are educators now, and they've dedicated much of their careers to understanding the lives of young people. I read their academic writing with great interest, but the personal stories they shared with me had an even greater impact on *A Song for Bijou*.

When I met with Toni, she told me about a funny instance of the word "Haitian" being misunderstood as "Asian," which I thought would be an amusing way to show Alex's ignorance of Bijou's cultural background. Toni also explained that spending time with a boy would have been next to impossible for a girl like Bijou, because until adulthood, girls are rarely more than a few steps away from a family member, teacher, priest, or other authority figure. I wanted to portray this as realistically as possible, but it posed a problem: if Bijou wouldn't be allowed to hang out with Alex, how would they ever get to know each other? And if my two main characters weren't able to spend time together, did I really have a book at all? The only solution was for Bijou and Alex to both become very creative, even deceptive, in order to be together. They're good, honest kids, but they want to get to know each other so badly that they're willing to bend a few rules along the way. I'm not saying lying to your parents is a good thing, but a fib or two in the service of love *is* a time-honored tradition that probably started a few thousand years before Shakespeare wrote *Romeo and Juliet*.

When I interviewed Fabienne, she told me she had learned English in Haiti largely by watching *All My Children* on satellite TV, and I found that detail too irresistible not to use for Bijou. More importantly, speaking with Fabienne influenced my decision that Bijou would be from a middle-class family—in Haiti, they would be called *bourgeois*—rather than a poorer one. While there are many different kinds of people from different economic backgrounds in Haiti, most Americans assume that all Haitians are desperately needy. This stereotype is one of many that Bijou confronts throughout the book; like so many newcomers to America, it is very hard for her to be truly seen by the kids she meets at her new school. Fabienne helped me to understand that.

Later, Gina Vellani, who coordinates the English as a Second Language instruction for thousands of Haitian students every year at Flatbush's essential resource center, CAMBA, allowed me to visit classes held on Church Avenue, just blocks away from Bijou's home in the book. While listening to Haitian ESL students introduce themselves and describe their lives in the English phrases they had learned only a few weeks earlier, I furiously scrawled notes on their diction and pronunciation. I also paid close attention to the way they dressed and used some of these details in describing Jou Jou and his bandmates.

Finally, I was aided greatly by a talented drummer in the Haitian tradition, Morgan Zwerlein, and a Brooklyn-based musicologist and musician, Lois Wilcken. Morgan helped me learn just enough hand-drumming technique to imagine what it would be like for Alex to study with Jou Jou. Lois helped me to understand the Haitian music scene in Brooklyn and told me all about the history of the Gran Bwa on the southern tip of Prospect Park, where anyone who wants to see some real-life rara should go on a Sunday afternoon between April and November. You will never forget what you see and hear there.